FAKE HOUSE

STORIES

FAKE HOUSE

STORIES

Linh Dinh

SEVEN STORIES PRESS

New York | London | Sydney | Toronto

Seven Stories Press
140 Watts Street
New York, NY 10013
http://www.sevenstories.com

In Canada:
Hushion House, 36 Northline Road, Toronto, Ontario M4B 3E2

In the U.K.:
Turnaround Publisher Services Ltd., Unit 3, Olympia Trading Estate, Coburg Road, Wood
Green, London N22 6TZ

In Australia:
Tower Books, 9/19 Rodborough Road, Frenchs Forest NSW 2086

Library of Congress Cataloging-in-Publication Data
Dinh, Linh, 1963-
Fake House/Linh Dinh.
p. cm.
ISBN 1-58322-039-9
1. Vietnam—Social life and customs—Fiction. 2. Vietnamese Americans—
Fiction. I. Title

PS3554.I494 F35 2000
813'.6—dc21
00-030802

9 8 7 6 5 4 3 2 1

College professors may order examination copies of Seven Stories Press titles for a free
six-month trial period. To order, visit www.sevenstories.com/textbook, or fax on school
letterhead to (212) 226-1411.

Book design by Adam Simon
Printed in the U.S.A.

to the unchosen

Stories in this collection have appeared in the following journals: "Fake House" in *VOLT*; "Uncle Tom's Cabin" in *New Observations*; "555" in *Threepenny Review*; "In the Vein" in *Witness*; "Two Who Forgot" in *Vietnam Review, Nhip Song*, and the Web journal *xconnect*; "Saigon Pull" in *New York Stories*; "Dead on Arrival" in *New American Writing*; "The Ugliest Girl" in *Insurance*; "Boo Hoo Hoo" in the Web journal *Editor's Picks*; "Fritz Glatman" and "Val" in *xconnect*. "Western Music" and "Fritz Glatman" have been anthologized in *Watermark: Vietnamese American Poetry and Prose*. Many of the stories have also been translated into Vietnamese by Phan Nhien Hao and published in *Hop Luu*.

CONTENTS

■ FAKE HOUSE

As I sit at my desk eating a ham sandwich (with mayo, no mustard), head bent over the sports section of the *Chronicle* (Dodgers 3, Giants 0), the phone rings. It's my wife: "Guess who just showed up?"

We haven't seen my brother Josh in over a year. "I'm really sorry," I say.

"Are you coming home early?"

"I… I will."

The last time he came, Josh stayed with us for over two weeks and didn't leave until I had given him a thousand dollars. "Good luck, Josh," I said as I left him at the Greyhound station.

"Thanks, Boffo."

Josh has called me "Boffo," short for "Boffo Mofo," since we were teenagers. He has always fancied himself to be some kind of a wordsmith. He also likes to draw pictures, blow into a saxophone.

Josh lives on the beach in Santa Monica. About six months ago I received a letter from him: "Dear Boffo, How are you? I was squatting in this warehouse with a bunch of people, very nice folks, mostly artists and musicians. We called it the Fake House (because it looked fake on the outside). It had running water but no shower and no electricity. To take a shower, you stood in a large trash can and scooped water from the sink and poured it on yourself. Everything was fine until three days ago. Mustapha—he's a painter—always left turpentine-soaked rags on the floor, and somebody must have dropped a cigarette on one of these rags because the place went up in flames! Poof! Just like that! No more Fake House! Now I sleep on the beach. I am ashamed to ask you this, but, Boffo, could you please send me two hundred dollars by Western Union? I'll pay you back when I can. Your brother, Josh. P.S. Please send my regards to Sheila." (My wife's name is "Sheilah," but Josh has always deleted the *h* from her name—yet another symptom of his overall slovenliness.) I thought, *There's no Fake House, no Mustapha, no fire,* but I sent him two hundred dollars anyway.

Aside from these begging letters, he also sends me post-cards from places you and I would never visit. One postmarked Salt Lake City said simply, "Ate flapjacks, saw pronghorns." One postmarked Belize City said, "Soggy Chinese food."

Why should I care that he ate flapjacks and saw pronghorns in Utah? That he had soggy Chinese food in Belize? But I suspect that for a man like Josh, who has accomplished nothing in this life, these trivial correspondences serve as confirmations that he exists, that he is doing something.

One year a flyer arrived around Christmas with a meticu-lously drawn image of Joseph Stalin in an awkward dancing pose, with this caption: *"No Party Like a Party Congress! Everybody Dances the Studder Steps!"*

"Tracy, I... I... I... I..." I am unable to finish my sentence. My secretary smiles. "You're stepping out, sir?"

I nod.

"You'll be back, sir?" I shake my head.

"You're going home, sir?"

I nod again, smile, and walk out of the office. There was an extra sparkle in Tracy's eyes. Perhaps she finds my stuttering, an absurd yet harmless defect, endearing. I've noticed that she has done something strange to her hair lately and that, since the weather has gotten warmer, she shows up most days for work in a curt, clingy dress and a clingy blouse made from a sheer fabric.

Aside from this small, perhaps endearing defect, I am a man in control of my own faculties and life. I manage two dozen residential units and four commercial buildings. Last year I cleared $135,000 after taxes. My wife does not have to do anything. She sits home and watches *Oprah,* takes tai chi lessons. A month ago she went to Hawaii alone.

I grip the steering wheel with my left hand and massage my left forearm with my right hand. Muscle tone is important. Time also. I do not like to waste time, even when driving. Then I switch hands, gripping the steering wheel with my right hand and massaging my right forearm with my left hand. Then I massage my right biceps while rotating my neck. "A clear road ahead!" I shout. As I drive, I like to reinforce my constitution with uplifting slogans. I never stutter when alone. "Firm but fair!" "Money is time!" Positive thoughts are an important component of my success. It is what separates me from those of my brother's ilk.

Occasionally, while driving, I'd surprise myself with an exuberant act of violence. Without premeditation my right hand would fly off the steering wheel and land flush on my right cheek. Whack! Afterward I'd feel a strange mixture of pride and humility, not because of the pain but because I had felt no pain.

I am in excellent shape for a man of forty-two. I have very little fat and no beer gut. With dinner I allow myself a single glass of chardonnay. Each morning before work I go to the spa and swim a dozen precise laps. Never thirteen. Never eleven. Then I stand still for about two minutes at the shallow end of the pool, with my eyes closed and my hands bobbing in the water, thinking about nothing. Mr. Chow, who is also at the pool early in the morning, has taught me this exercise. After watching me swim, he said: "You have too much yang. You must learn how to cultivate your ying." Or maybe it was the other way around: "You have too much ying. You must learn how to cultivate your yang." In any case he suggested that I stand still at the shallow end of the pool for a couple of minutes each day, breathe in deeply, exhale slowly, and think about nothing.

It is very relaxing, this exercise, but of course, no one can ever think about nothing. As I stand still at the shallow end of the pool, what I must do for the rest of the day comes sharply into focus: *Send eviction notice to 2B, 245 Montgomery. Jack up rent from 600 to 625 on new lease for 2450 Anna Drive. The idiot on the third floor at 844 Taylor has dumped paper towel into the toilet again, flooding the basement. Call plumber. Send bill to idiot….*

Josh is my only sibling. He is a year older than me. He is my older brother. When we were kids, Josh was considered by our parents to be by far the smarter one, someone who would surely leave his mark on the world, a prediction he took quite seriously. But the facts have proven otherwise. I have often thought the reason I tolerate these visits by my loser brother, during which he never behaves graciously but often vulgarly, atrociously, and at the end of which I will have to part with a thousand dollars, or at least five hundred bucks, is because he is tangible proof that I have not failed in this life. I'm not a loser. I am not Josh. We have the same background, grew up in the same idiotic city, San Mateo, raised by the same quarrelsome parents, a garrulous, megalomaniacal father and a childish, know-nothing mother. Josh was considered by all to be the smarter one, even the better-looking one. Although we started out with roughly the same handicaps, I was never afflicted by his hubris, never thought I had to leave a so-called mark on this world. I never wanted to be better than people, although, such is life, I am now doing better than just about anyone I know (and certainly better than everyone I grew up with), whereas Josh, who was so convinced of his superiority, has degenerated into a pathetic loser, taking showers in trash cans and living under the same roof with people with names like Mustapha.

It is true that my brother is better-looking than me. Girls were enthralled by him. He lost his virginity at fifteen. I at twenty-three. But as he grew older, this superficial asset became increasingly worthless. Mature women do not care for good looks and a glib conversation. What they want is a roof over their head, a breadwinner, and a father for their children. They like to be warm and clean. What woman will put up with standing in a trash can and having water poured over herself? Although Sheilah and I do not have children, we will when the time is right. There is no hurry.

It is a shame you cannot see my wife because any man who has will concede that she is a strikingly, almost disturbingly, beautiful woman. She has eyes that beg a little but lips that are determined, fierce, without being vulgar or cruel. They are well drawn and not too fleshy. Her smiles are discreet. She is not one of those women who, out of fear and dishonesty, are constantly showing their teeth. She is tall, two, maybe three inches taller than me.

Sheilah is Tracy's predecessor. She worked for me for two years before we started dating. It was she who asked me out the first time. The pretext was her twenty-fourth birthday. She said, "Me and a bunch of friends are going to this French bistro on Ghirardelli Square for my birthday. Would you like to come as my date?"

I noticed she had said "date," not "friend." She did not say, "Would you like to come as my friend?" but "Would you like to come as my date?" *Here's that crack in the line,* I thought, *run for it.*

I must admit that although I was attracted to Sheilah from the moment she walked into my office for the job interview, I did not dare to betray my interest. She was out of my league. Even now, five years into our marriage, I still catch myself in moments of self-congratulation. Once I even laughed out loud, shaking my head and exclaiming, "You didn't do too bad, you ugly son of a bitch!"

Josh, on the other hand, has never been married, has never even had a relationship with a woman lasting more than a few months. Three times he had to borrow money from me to pay for his girlfriends' abortions. It is a good thing, these abortions, considering the kind of father he would have made.

I haven't told you about the incident that prompted me to get rid of him the last time he came to stay with us.

He had been brooding in front of the TV all week, drunk on my wine. When he wanted to borrow my car one night to go into town, I was more than happy to oblige. I even gave him twenty dollars for beer. He left at eight o'clock and came back at around one in the morning. I could tell immediately that he had a girl with him. My wife was asleep but as usual I was up reading. Each night before bed I try to take in at least twelve pages of a good novel. Although a businessman, I do not neglect to develop the left side of my brain. On that night, if I remember correctly, I was reading *The Joy Luck Club* by Maxine Hong Kingston.

Since the guest room is adjacent to the master bedroom, I could hear their voices fairly distinctly. Josh was talking in a near whisper, but the girl was loud. She was black. I could never recall him dating an African-American girl or showing any interest in black women, and was a little surprised by this fact. Of course playing the saxophone, he was always listening to the great black musicians. They were haggling.

"Please."

"You don't got forty bucks?"

"I only have ten."

"Uh-uh."

"I'll give you my jacket." It was actually a ski jacket I had lent him.

"I won't even suck your motherfuckin' white-trash dick for that motherfuckin' boo sheeiiit jacket!"

"Please."

"Get me the fuck out of here!"

She left.

It was over in less than a minute. I was so startled by such an unusual incident occurring in my own home that I had no time to react. Maybe I was a little disappointed that something even more bizarre did not happen. My wife had slept through the entire episode. She could sleep through anything: car alarms, sirens, earthquakes. I looked down at her serene, distant face and felt an overwhelming urge to penetrate.

A week, maximum, I decide, massaging my right thigh as I turn into the driveway. We live in a split-level three-bedroom house with a two-car garage, in an upscale, multi-ethnic neighborhood. My brother is standing inside the plate glass window of the living room, waiting for me. He has on a dirty-looking baseball cap and a black T-shirt. When he comes out of the house, I notice that he has put on weight just in the past year. He has never taken care of his body, never eaten right, never exercised. He trots down the sloping brick path leading to my car, smiling shamelessly. My brother is always most obsequious during the first few days. Sheilah is nowhere to be seen. I step out of the car. "Good to see you, Boffo!" he practically screams. We hug.

"How… how… how are you?"

"Can't complain!"

"Howsa, howsa… Mustapha?"

Josh looks confused. Then he says, "Mustapha died in the fire."

A professional con man, my brother. I place a hand on the back of his neck and start to massage it without thinking. I lead him into my house.

■ FRITZ GLATMAN

Mariechelle, Norie, Loida, Sylvana, Emie, Dulce, Maria, Marites…. The catalogue, *Origami Geishas,* is laid out like the cheapest high school yearbook. Twenty-four out-of-focus black-and-white photographs to a newsprint page. Thirty-two pages. Six-hundred-plus brown women desiring a white man who will take her into his home.

```
     LBFM-168 Geniva (19) Philippines/ 5-
3; 103; domestic helper (some college).
"Frankly I long for male friend with no
vice, a strong sense of humour, believe
in Our Saviour. I am kind-hearted, sim-
pleminded, and sincere. I like bowling."

     LBFM-352 Consorcia (28) Malaysia
(Filipina)/4-10; 95; agri-
forester/zoologist. "I like soft music,
Thoreau, dancing, cooking. I like a man
who is easy to go along, no back
talking. I am interested in soul mates,
some drinking, not too much."
```

```
     LBFM-577 Goldnar (21) Hong Kong
(Filipina)/5-0; 100; student; Catholic.
"I am lovable."
```

I am Fritz Glatman (43), American, of English and Austrian extractions/6-1; 227; of Counsel at the Center City law firm of Gontarek & Enfield. I am divorced, with no children. My ex, Jane Kulik, was recently made a partner at Cohen, Javens, Petaccia & Kulik. We've been exchanging Christmas cards every year for the past fourteen years.

Within the past year I've been toying with the idea of securing for myself an Asian woman, a mail-order bride. I've been brooding over this prospect, sober or drunk, on many sleepless nights. *A hoary wet dream,* I'd think, emitting a little laugh. A last-ditch recourse. *Aegri somnia.*

This solution plunged me into the deepest shame initially, but I am now increasingly resigned to its feasibility. There's even a dull excitement daily creeping up on me.

Before this idée fixe, if you will, took hold, I was never partial to Asian women. Never even thought about them. But with mental exertion came a gradual, grudging appreciation. Stare at anything long enough, I suppose, and beauty will rise to the surface.

The girls in *Origami Geishas* are mostly plain, their faces plain, their hair plain. Some are outright ugly. But my future wife must be unequivocally beautiful, though not too beautiful. Son of an immigrant, I was taught to be modest, to shy away from luxuries, and to shun all ostentatious displays. Indeed, even with a six-figure salary, I drive an old-model Ford.

But I should quantify that she must be at least several notches better-looking than I am. Like any man, I cannot be satisfied with merely an equitable return for my pecuniary investment. I want a little extra.

She need not be too smart obviously. If I want to feed my brain, I'll buy a book. What it comes down to is this: I can only exchange what I have, money, and the fact that I'm a citizen of a first-world country, for what she has, what every woman has.

My wife will undoubtedly be a social incongruity in my life, a foul ball and a blip on my record. I'm a lawyer, not a sailor for Uncle Sam. But since it would not be feasible to conceal her existence from my colleagues, to lock her up, figuratively speaking, in a carriage house or a wine cellar, sentence her to life without parole, or to introduce her as an au pair—or, rather, as a maid—to my neighbors, I must steel myself for the negative publicity, from the invidious snickers to righteous smirks to actionable slanders. Caveat emptor.

To facilitate her assimilation into this society, perhaps it is advisable that I send her to the community college for a semester or two of remedial English, art, and music appreciation, and to let her wallow in the secure ambience of a college campus.

My father, long dead, would not have objected to my marrying an Asian woman. A kind-hearted, simpleminded, and sincere man, he was a concrete contractor for forty-odd years, specializing in driveways, patios, handicapped ramps, and stucco. Although he never finished high school, he was an enthusiastic reader. He pronounced *Orientals* "Orienals." He would lecture to his five children: "The Orienals are an inward people. I have a lot of respect for them. They have an inward orienation because of their physiognomy. The epicanthic folds on their eyes block out much of the sun, and hence much of the world. They have a wispy physique, and do not gorge themselves on red meat like we do. They live on top of each other, in gross discomfort, which drives them further inward. Because they have no outer space"—he would hush his voice at this point, squint his eyes—"they must seek inner space. They live close to the earth, build flat houses, and are small of stature."

He had a peculiar concept called perpendicularity. Angles and curves had to be minimized. All the furniture in our house, beds, tables, were lined up at a ninety-degree angle to the wall, hugging it, with the middle of the floor kept empty. Throw rugs were banished, since they could not be maintained at right angles. At dinner, forks and knives, when at rest, had to be placed perpendicular to the edge of the table. Likewise, if our chairs were not perpendicular to the edge of the table as we were eating, he would whack us on the head. Do not lean against the wall, he always reminded us. "The Orientals sit at round tables," he said. "They have no sense of perpendicularity."

A minor problem: I've been advised that the Filipinos cannot enunciate the "f" sound. They call their own country "Pilippines." It is perhaps the only country in the world that cannot pronounce its own name. Instead of "Fritz," my wife would have to call me "Pritz."

Naturally, in thinking about my future wife, I've become more alert to all things Asian. At least three times a week you'll find me at some restaurant in Chinatown, happily stuffing my face with sashimis, happy pancakes, spring rolls, or wontons. I'm conditioning my innards for her cooking. I asked Justin Park (né Duk Chong Park), a new associate at our firm, for book recommendations. We were standing by the Mr. Coffee: "Justin, I've been thinking a lot about Southeast Asia recently, the Philippines in particular. I want to take a trip there next year. Never been to Asia. Can you recommend a book for me to read?"

"I'm Korean, Fritz."

"I know, buddy, I know! Duck Pork is a Korean name! Pusan City. I've seen your résumé. But if anyone here knows anything about Asia, you do, so don't be so defensive."

"All right, all right, there's a novel by Jessica Hagedorn called *Dogeaters*."

"Dogeaters?!"

"Yes, *Dogeaters*."

"Is it any good? What's it about?"

"It's pretty good"—he furrowed his brows, tried to remember the book—"but it's hard to summarize it. There's too many characters. It's about Manila. There's a guy named Joey Sands, a half-black, half-Filipino hustler, and a fat German film director, a Fassbinder type whom the hustler called Rain or Shine."

"That's pretty clever: Rainer, Rain or Shine!" He was trying to get back at me for being a Kraut, I could tell.

Justin has been with us for just over a year. Fresh from Harvard Law, he does fairly good work but is perceived by the other attorneys as being a tad too cocky. As the firm's first minority hire, however, his job is reasonably secure. He wears a loud tie not only on Fridays but on every other day as well. While standing in the elevator lobby, he often shoots an invisible basketball at an invisible hoop, throws an invisible football at an invisible receiver, or swings an invisible bat at an invisible baseball. He pulls these stunts even in the presence of clients. But in spite of this showy proclivity for sports, he declined to join our softball team. After he became adjusted to his new surroundings, as his confidence grew, he went out and got both of his ears pierced. He was sleeping with one of the temps, a petite twenty-two-year-old named Traci Mintz, a clone of Shannon Miller, the gymnast who broke her ankle on TV. They were often seen leaving TGIF together. It is none of my business, of course, but our firm is fairly small, with only twelve attorneys. After Traci left, he started to pork our beloved, longtime receptionist, Julia LaPorte, a buxom widow in her late thirties.

A week after our chat about the Philippines, Justin said, "Fritz, I don't mean to be nosy, but, ah, are you thinking about getting yourself a mail-order bride?"

I stared at him in disbelief. What chutzpah! Doesn't this punk know what privacy is? "Whoa! Ha! ha! That's pretty funny. Why would you say that?"

"Just asking."

I looked him straight in the eyes, tried not to blink too fast: "I'm going to the Philippines because I want to see Asia: a guy like me, forty-three years old, never seen Asia. It's the biggest continent in the world, you know, all those people, ha! ha! I can't afford Korea. Or Japan. Or Singapore. And Vietnam: all those bad associations. And I also have, uh, this interest in volcanoes. I grew up in Washington State, I don't know if you know that, near Mount St. Helens. She popped her top fifteen years ago, remember?" He was blank. "Maybe you weren't even here then. But there's this one spectacular volcano in the Philippines called, uh"—I couldn't think of its damn name—"it's on the tip of my tongue. What is it, what is it, what's the name of that volcano?"

It was a dreadful performance, and I'm sure he saw right through me. Maybe I can figure out a way to get him fired before I bring my bride over.

Sitting in Chinatown restaurants, surrounded by Asians

laughing and yakking away as they eat, I've come to realize that they are simply more forthright about life's amenities than we are. There is a recently released film directed by this Chinese guy, Ang Lee, called *Eat, Drink, Man, Woman.* I didn't see the film, but I know what the title means: Eat, drink, man, woman.

Then there is this other film called *The Ballad of Nagasaki,* by a guy named Arakawa. In it there was this Japanese hick who had just lost his wife. The entire village helped him to find a new wife. She arrived from the next village, sight unseen. First thing she did was stuff her face with potatoes, she was starving, then she lay next to him. They had sex without saying a word to each other. Afterwards he said, "I feel much better."

When I go to The Office, a go-go bar on Fifteenth Street, I see men from all over, a veritable assembly of the United Nations. Nowhere else can I hobnob so freely with Pakistanis, blacks, and Mongolians. Each man nursing an inconsolable hard-on, wearing a shroud of pussies, we are all humbled, pared down, incorporated. We must all share the nude girl hanging upside down from the greased pole. She's presently doing a series of queer sit-ups to polite applause. None of us can have her. The best we can do is to give her a dollar. It is the most democratic place on earth. All the sexual surplus of society ends up in a go-go bar; it's where men go to celebrate their equality. I'm reminded of a Cézanne painting called *The Eternal Female,* in which men of various professions and pretensions, high and low, are depicted gazing up at a naked woman hovering over their heads.

Apropos of prostitution and pornography, a symbolic defilement of intimacy and a séance of lovemaking, respectively: I would never patronize a whore because I cannot consent to sex without commitment, with neither preface nor prologue, but neither will I allow myself to be titillated, or moved to the depths of my soul, by a photo of a naked female, the cheapest form of idolatry. (Masturbation, which is unavoidable, I consider a breathing exercise, a cardiovascular fitness program, a trip into the future and a jogging of the memory. Time traveling.) I avert my eyes from lingerie ads in the newspaper. If I must read an article on the same page as the ad, I cover the exposed flesh with a book or a bagel.

A remedy to the aforesaid perversions, of course, is the go-go bar. In front of me is a real woman, after all, doing what all women do, one way or another. She is alert to my presence, as I am to hers. We have a relationship. The slightest shift in mood in either party is duly registered by the other, a yawn, a pitying smile, a hardening of the facial features betraying irritation or disappointment.

But I must admit that any relationship I can have with a woman in a go-go bar is bound to be unbalanced, asymmetrical. I've thought a lot about this. To start with: she's naked, and I'm not. While she could only read my face, I could read her entire body. Because clothing serves to isolate the face, a naked woman, in shedding her clothes, surrenders her right, the right of any civilized human being, to frame her own face. If I was with a clothed woman, that is, with a framed face, I would gauge her fluctuating moods primarily by deciphering her facial expressions. I may scrutinize her other exposed flesh, but I could only do it on the sly, in piecemeal fashion, because of the tyranny of her face.

When a woman is naked, however, her face loses its authority. Now I'm free to look wherever I please. Now I'm free, even compelled, to look away from her face. And because I'm not really paying attention to her face but seeing it only out of the corner of my eye, it can no longer cajole, curb, pace, or ridicule my responses to her. The rest of her body is mute, blind, and cannot censor my curiosity.

Also: because she is being probed simultaneously by so many sets of eyes, not just mine, what I'm doing, what all the other men are doing, becomes less selfish and subjective, less perverted, and more universal and scientific. We're on a joint expedition to a far-away land, a field trip to the zoo.

All that said, it must be added that a woman's naked body can never betray as much as a man's. Hers is a mask, with the nipples the eyes peeping through the eye holes, the only indicator of tension within. With a man, on the other hand, every psychic tic or turbulence is conveyed immediately by an erection, or at least half an erection. Anything at all can cause a man to have an erection. One can say that his body is more guileless and articulate than hers: a blunt instrument, it always speaks its mind. For a man, clothing serves the absolutely essential purpose of hiding his erections.

The idea itself, of procuring a mail-order bride, can be traced to the fact that a friend of mine from undergraduate school married a Chinese woman two years ago. The pale pink wedding invitation arrived in the mail. Brian Panzram will be wedded to Josie Woo. I called Brian up. I said, "So, Brian, who's this Josie Woo?"

Then Lafcadio Kerns, an associate at our firm, showed up with a Thai girl at last year's Christmas party. She was much, much too beautiful for someone like Laffy, a squat fellow with a beer belly and eyes dilating in two directions. I was standing next to Justin by the hors d'oeuvres table. "Check out Laffy's squeeze," I said.

Justin crammed a slice of pâté-smeared bruschetta into his mouth, chewed it with his mouth open. "Yeah?"

"That's not right."

He chuckled, flushed his mouth with martini.

"Look at her!"

"Relax, Fritz."

"Look at him!"

"You think she's that hot?"

"Are you blind?!"

"She's all right."

"Every man should have a girl that pretty. How come you're not with a Chinese girl?"

"I would ask an Asian girl out for a date if I were white."

An odd thing for him to say, I thought. I even thought he had said, "I would ask an Asian girl out for a date if only I were white," but then that really wouldn't make any sense.

"And why do you care?" he continued.

"Never mind, never mind," I waved him off and walked away.

The music was vibrating the floor. I went to the bar and said, "Give me some of that Puligny whatever." The grinning bartender tilted the heavy bottle over my trembling flute. I drank it in one gulp, spilling half of it on my shirt. *It's time to leave,* I decided.

I sidled along the wall, dodging the tuxedoed and black-dressed figures convulsing to the techno music. This ape-din, why do people listen to it?

I almost made it to the door when Laffy intercepted me. "Yo, Fritz!" He was hoisting a bottle of Cristal over his nearly bald head, spilling champagne all over it, a drunken gloat. One of his hands appeared surgically sewn to his girlfriend's bare midriff.

"I've got to go. I've got to go." I tried to ward him off.

"I'd like you to meet Grace."

"Nice to meet you, Grace," I extended my hand, "I'm Fritz Glatman."

"I'm Grace."

"Grace what?"

"Grace Kittikasem."

"What's that? Thai?"

"Very good," she said, with discernible disdain in her voice. *If only we were alone, you fuckin' bitch, I'd teach you some American manners.* Laffy was frowning at me, his eyes dilating in two directions. It was all I could do to refrain myself from punching him in the face.

■ THE UGLIEST GIRL

My consciousness begins with the fact that I'm an ugly girl. And not just any ugly girl but the ugliest girl. Not counting the freaks, the harelips, the Down's syndromes, the ones with lye splashed on their face, born without a nose, an extra mouth, five ears, and so on, I am the ugliest girl.

When I cross the street in front of a car, I always stare straight ahead and never look in the driver's direction. I do not want to startle him with my ugliness. Even in my dreams I do this: avert my gaze from the driver as I cross the street.

At a party, should there be another ugly girl in the room—perhaps someone only half as ugly as I am—it would be me who would be embarrassed. I would be embarrassed for her because as soon as she sees me, I become her mirror. By being there, I expose her, interfere with her attempt to pass. My presence would ground her.

Without me there is a possibility that she could forget, for a moment, who she is. Surrounded by beautiful people, she might even lapse into the illusion that she is one of them, that she belongs to them and not to her own ugliness.

But with me in the room, this possibility is eliminated. Suddenly there is a subgroup, a minority of two, a sorority of ugliness.

An ugly face does not transcend, cannot transcend: it is made of mud. Molded on a wobbly potter's wheel, it has no structural integrity. An ugly face descends, points downward. It is collapsible yet heavy. It is something soggy, macerated, on the verge of falling apart. All diseases lurk beneath its skin. It gives off a stench one can smell even in a photograph.

A beautiful face adheres to five, maybe six models, whereas an ugly face can shoot off in any direction. Ugliness is inventive, restless, adventurous, promiscuous.

The slightest misplacement of a nose or an eye—say by 1/32 of an inch—can produce the most insidious effects. An ugly face is a parody, not of a beautiful face but of ugliness.

A beautiful face will be forgiven for all inanities and cruelties spewing from its mouth—even vomit from a beautiful face is a turn-on—but an ugly face will be held accountable for even the smallest indiscretion.

The life of a face is capricious. Even the most subtle shift in lighting or mood—in either subject or object—can transform a beautiful face into an ugly one. This said, it is true that a genuinely ugly face can never appear beautiful under any circumstance.

A man who falls in love with an ugly woman will never be able to forgive her for his degradation. All of his rationalizations will be useless. Shocked and humiliated, he will think, *My God, what am I doing?* before he exacts his revenge on her.

The revulsion caused by an ugly face is tempered by pity and indifference. Whatever violence it may induce is different in kind from that which is aroused by a beautiful face.

Great beauty enrages. It disturbs. Great beauty invites desecration.

There is a photograph of me at five years old. There are eight of us, all girls. At the front, in a pink-and-white-striped dress, and standing with her legs wide apart, is Kelley Henchey. She's the most beautiful. That's why she's front and center. The rest of us huddle behind her. I'm at the back, my face hidden behind the right shoulder of Linda Oakes, with only the top of my head visible.

The adults did not pose us. We posed ourselves. Even at five I knew.

As kids we would play "Spin the Bottle." We would all sit in a circle around an empty soda bottle. The bottle would be spun and whoever the bottle pointed to consecutively would have to kiss each other.

I was included in this game only to add suspense to the proceeding. The boys kissed me stoically, bravely—some even pretended to enjoy it. Steve Breitenfeld made a point of sticking his tongue in my mouth, shocking all those present. We were both eleven. In seventh grade I sat in the gym bleachers during sock-hops and watched as my friends rubbed their bodies cautiously against boys during the slow numbers. I thought of the possibility of my being a lifelong virgin, and of becoming a nun or a lesbian.

But then I had my first sexual experience.

The Wainwrights lived next door to us. When Mr. Wainwright mowed his lawn, he would mow ours also, we were such good neighbors. They had two kids: Lauren, who was my age—we were both twelve—and Jason, who had just entered college and was seventeen.

It was New Year's and I was over at their house. Jason was watching a football game. He was sprawled on the carpet with a can of beer in his hand. No adults were around. Lauren and I were pretending to be cheerleaders. We would shout, "Michigan, yahoo!" and kick our legs up. At one point Lauren said, "Jason, I want to stand on your shoulders."

Jason lifted Lauren up onto his shoulders. Lauren said, "Rah! Rah!" and Jason said, "Rah! Rah!" and then Jason let his sister down and said to me, "Now, Becky, your turn!"

He crouched down so that I could climb onto his shoulders. I sort of squatted on his shoulders, then rose slowly, my hands holding his hands. After I stood up straight, he placed a hand behind my buttocks to help me keep my balance. I gasped because his hand was right against my panties—I was wearing a skirt. Lauren pretended she didn't see this. She said nothing. No one said anything. Aside from the noise from the TV there was no other noise in the room. We all pretended to be watching TV. Everyone held their breath. Without looking up at me, Jason slipped his thumb under my panties. At first he didn't do anything. He just kept his thumb there. Then he pressed and pressed, trying to find the point of entry. Then he started to wiggle it. I stood perfectly still while he wiggled his thumb inside me. Lauren could no longer contain herself. She turned to us and yelled, "Stop!"

Jason put me down.

Little did I know that this would be a precedent. All of my erotic adventures, from that point on, would be arrived at fraudulently, by accident, pilfered from drunken, nearly unconscious men. A sexual shoplifter, I would never have sex as sex, only its double. While others can seek their pleasures out in the open, I must seek mine underground, through stealth and corruption, through substitutions and perversions.

I even thought of travel as a solution. In Antananarivo, Vishakhapatnam, or Ulan Bator, a white girl (with blond hair, blue eyes), even one as ugly as I am, would be an exotic creature, and hence desirable.

In Idfu or Maroni. In Fuzhou. In Kyushu or Lagash. In Kigali.

I would come into McGlinchey's and see a man sitting by himself. If he was an ugly man, someone fat or old or with other obvious defects, or a foreigner, an Indian or a Chinese, someone socially crippled, unglamorous, or a black man, I would send him a drink. Surprised that a woman was buying him a drink, he would look over and smile, think things over and most likely ignore me. After a while I would send him a second, then a third drink. Some would be so disgusted they would not even look in my direction after the second drink. Some would leave the bar. But there are also those who would reciprocate by buying me a drink. A few would come over and sit next to me.

Once, as I was leaving the bar, I heard, "I wouldn't fuck her with your dick and me pushing." It was the bouncer talking to one of his buddies. It is a tedious job, being a bouncer, and he usually has a friend standing by him to keep him company most of the night. As I walked down the street, I thought, *Did he actually say that? He couldn't possibly have said that. He seems like a friendly guy and I'm always nice to him. Maybe he said, "I wouldn't hug her because she's sick and it's catching." Or maybe he was talking about somebody else.*

I also thought that although what he said was in itself malicious, his tone was jocular, friendly, even endearing. He did not intend to wound. To separate content from delivery is a sign of madness. Besides, it was simply a statement of sexual preference. You can't force someone to find you attractive. Desire is fickle. And he was not talking to me but to a buddy. Anything could have triggered such a remark: boredom, the desire to amuse, even flirtatiousness.

I was already three blocks from the bar when I decided to go back and confront him. It was a mistake. As soon as I barged through the door, as soon as the bouncer and his buddy saw me again, what had been said earlier, even if it was directed at somebody else, would now be applicable to me. Both of them must have thought, since the sentence was still fresh in their minds, *I wouldn't fuck her with your dick and me pushing.*

A man would say, "Looks like shit, feels great."

A man would say, "That girl *requires* two six-packs."

One night as I sat at the bar, a midget bumped against my elbow. I hadn't even noticed him until his head bumped against my elbow.

It was after midnight and the place was packed. The midget stood patiently waiting to be served. When the bartender came over, the midget said, "What do you have to do get service around here?"

"First you have to be able to see over the bar. What you want?"

"A Rolling Rock."

I burst out laughing. The midget also laughed. He said to me, "How you doing?"

It was very loud in there. I shouted, "I'm all right. How are you?"

He shouted back, "Can I buy you a drink?"

"Sure."

The midget was about twenty-five, with a smart-alecky face. He had a very deep voice, the voice of a seven-footer. When the bartender came back, the midget said, "Sir, can you get her a drink also?"

I didn't like his face hovering below my breast. I said, "You want to share my seat?"

"No, no, that's all right."

"No, really." I scooted my ass over.

He hopped up. "I'm Spanky."

"I'm Becky."

We sat in silence, minding our drinks. His bony hip rubbed against mine. He started to rock back and forth, his feet dangling, then stopped, as if suddenly realizing the inappropriateness of what he was doing. On his square head, flakes of dandruff, like dried onion, were impaled by strands of thinning yellow hair. He said, "You want a shot?"

"I don't drink shots."

"A martini? A mixed drink?"

"I'll take a Jack and Ginger."

"What is your name again?"

"Becky!"

"I'm Spanky!" Then to the bartender: "Sir, can you give Becky a Jack and Ginger, and an Absolut for me?"

I said, "Absolut… yuck! The last time I drank Absolut, I threw up the whole next day."

"Where do you live?" The midget placed his left hand on my right knee.

I thought, *How did we get from me throwing up to "Where do you live?"* I did not answer him. He became frightened and took his hand away. I smiled earnestly to reassure him. I leaned my face forward in a vague gesture of intimacy. Our drinks arrived. We toasted: "Cheers!" A generic toast. He placed his left hand on my right knee again. He rubbed this hand back and forth.

Two drinks later his hand was palming my inner thigh. It was like a catcher's mitt someone had forgotten. He kept it immobile. He didn't want me to think about it: that his hand was between my legs. If I could have given him my pussy in a plastic bag, he would have said, "Thank you," kissed me good night, and walked out the door. I said, "Let's go."

"Let go?"

"No, no, let's get out of here."

A man that hard up could easily turn out violent. The whole time I was talking to him, I was thinking of the word *dire*.

A couple had yanked my hair in bed. One had punched me

in the face. But this guy was only a midget. He was half my size. He was a midget.

As we walked down Locust, Spanky couldn't stop rubbing my ass with his hand. Now pinching, now stroking, he wanted to get as much he could just in case I changed my mind. He was praying. He wanted to rake it all in and save up for the future.

At an intersection, as we waited for the light to change, he steered his face toward my pelvis and jabbed his nose at my crotch. Many cars drove by. Some people honked their horns. I said, "Spanky, you're treating me like a whore."

He ignored me. He was homebound and could no longer be distracted. A car slowed and a frat boy with his head sticking out the window yelled: "Whoooooooooosh!!!!"

He burrowed and burrowed and burrowed. He gnawed. He clawed my ass with both hands as he bit my denims. He unzipped me with his teeth.

■ VAL

1. What Patricia Saw in Trenton

Last month I was in Trenton waiting for the train to Philadelphia. There were maybe twenty people standing on the platform. A woman to my left, her back turned to me, was wearing a yellow sweat shirt, embroidered with the cartoon character Scooby Doo, over a print dress patterned with dancing chili peppers—a chili-spangled dress. She had on Dr. Martens boots. She was very tall, about five-ten, with dirty-blond hair. Something about her posture was oddly familiar: feet spread wide, groin tucked back, belly out, gravity centered. Her meaty hands were clasped behind her back over her non-buttocks. Did I know this woman?

When she turned sideways, I checked out her profile: small yet lumpy nose; pointy chin; round, protruding forehead—all in all, not a very attractive woman. And then it dawned on me: it was Valentino! a boy I once dated for five tumultuous months three years ago. Rather than risking an encounter, I went back inside the station. I don't think he saw me.

2. Val Washing Dishes

From the time I was twelve to the time I left home at the age of seventeen, my two household chores were (1) taking the garbage out once a week; and (2) washing the dishes on Monday, Wednesday, Friday, and Sunday (my mother took care of the other days). Although I did not mind either chore, I particularly enjoyed washing dishes. I would stand at the sink, with my feet spread wide, my groin tucked back, my belly out, gravity centered, sponge in hand, and go to work. I enjoyed the contact of suds on skin and never wore those faggoty pale pink latex rubber gloves. I was an exceptionally competent dishwasher, maybe the best ever, with a clean repertoire of hand movements to minimize expenditure of time and detergent. The objective was to eradicate grease and food scum from each vessel without abrading the aluminum on a frying pan or tarnishing the tender glaze of a fragile tea cup. You do not want to injure your dishes. Dishwashing is a civilizing act. It's not just a coda and bookend to eating but a counterbalance, nay, a refutation, to its organic consequence. At the end of each session, as a reward for a job well done, I would keep my hands beneath the faucet, under very hot water, for maybe a minute.

There was a risk to this indulgence, however. Sometimes I would be so transported by hot water running over my hands that I would stand there for not one but two minutes. That's when evil thoughts would seep into my consciousness. I would think, for example, of pulling my pants down, right there in the kitchen, with my mother watching TV a few feet away in the living room. (She wouldn't have been able to see me, but, still, she was only a few feet away.) Or, worse, I would think of stabbing myself with the still-wet bread knife sticking out of the dish rack.

She's watching TV in the living room, alone. Dad is upstairs in his study. I can hear the sounds of recorded laughs and a man's voice saying, "But, Margaret, you didn't!" "But of course I did, Henry." "You mean you didn't tell me it was all a misunderstanding?" More recorded laughs. My hands are pink under the hot water. Mom thinks I'm still washing dishes. I have unzipped my fly to allow my half-erect penis to stick out of my jeans. I can smell the musk of my own sex. Only with a superhuman effort can I refrain from taking the still-wet bread knife sticking out of the dish rack and stabbing myself over and over, over and over. Ha! ha! More recorded laughs.

3. The Father

When I heard what my son had done, I nearly had a heart attack. I mean, how can anyone, no matter how deranged, do that to himself?! It's unheard of. It was my wife, Trish, who had answered the phone. She walked into my study, pale as a radish, with her eyes shut tight.

"What happened, Trish?"

"Oh God, oh my God, oh God, oh my God…" She was shaking her head from side to side, her mouth wide open, her eyes shut tight.

"Say it!"

"Oh God, oh my God, oh God, oh my God…"

"Say it!"

"Oh God, oh my God, oh God, oh my God…"

It was sickening…. Trish flew to Philadelphia right away to see Val, but I stayed behind. I went to work the next day as if nothing had happened. I didn't know how to broach the subject to anyone. I couldn't say, for example, "Val got into an accident, and Trish flew to Philadelphia to see him."

But I should have gone with her, I should have. Maybe I was too afraid to see him, to look him in the eyes, knowing what I knew.

Are Trish and I responsible? What did we do to cause this disaster?

In elementary school, a few kids did call him Valerie. Maybe I shouldn't have named him Valentino.

4. Spokane International to Philadelphia International via O'Hare

It was a seven-hour plane ride and I was crying the whole time. The stewardess said, "Are you okay, ma'am?" I bit my lip and nodded. I couldn't even speak. The elderly gentleman next to me was trying hard to ignore my distress.

And all this time my husband and I had thought Val was finally getting his act together. He was going out with a girl. Patty, her name was, Patricia Potemkin. What did she do to him?

It was not a good sign that Patty was eight years older than my son. But considering the fact that Val never dated in high school, never even went to a dance, we were glad he had found somebody. We wanted to raise an upright gentleman, yes, not a homosexual.

But I never did like the way she looked. In the one photograph Val sent us, she was wearing shades, a black leather vest over white T-shirt, black leather pants, and black boots. A girl who is that self-conscious about her appearance has got to be bad news, I had thought. She had almost no lips and her teeth were extremely large.

"You think they're sexually active?" I had asked my husband.

"How would I know?"

"But what do you think?"

"If you're so curious, why don't you ask him?"

"I can't ask him, I'm his mother. You ask him."

"They're probably doing it right now, Trish, as we're talking! He's twenty-four, for God's sake!"

5. The Sun Deck

We had a sun deck at the back of our house. It was about twelve feet off the ground. It overhung, on two sides, a cement-paved patio, and on one side, a flowerbed: gloxinia, morning glories, and black-eyed Susans Mom had planted.

One of my earliest memories was of me and Dad standing on the sun deck pissing on the flowerbed.

6. Puberty

When I was thirteen, straight strands of hair jutted out from the hypogastric region above my uncircumcised penis. I took out a scissors and cut them off. They reappeared. This time I not only cut them off with a scissors but shaved my entire pubic region. Again they reappeared.

But then I thought, *Hmm, maybe these strands will grow so thick they'll hide my penis!* I waited a month for this to happen.

A big letdown: The hairs grew but were so sparse they hid nothing.

But then I had a brilliant idea.

I had had in my possession a Thomas Eakins black-and-white photograph of a female nude in which the crotch area was shadowy, almost black. Whenever I looked at this fudgy, smudgy area of the photograph, I would get an erection. On the other hand, more explicit photographs, those in colors and featuring exposed genitals, had always repulsed me.

I stood naked ten feet away from a full-length mirror. The curtains were drawn and the lights had been turned off. I had rubbed black shoe polish on my penis and testicles and all around my pubic area. In the mirror there was nothing but shadow between my legs.

But then something unexpected happened. My rising black erection rose above this shadow area.

You may not believe this, but I NEVER masturbated as a teenager. I did not know what masturbation was. I did not know that you're supposed to stroke up and down.

7. T-shirt Games

Game #1: Retract both arms from armholes of T-shirt. Keep elbows close to sides. Place fists in front of chest. *Voilà!* Now you have a beautiful pair of breasts.

Game #2: Imagine that many people are watching you as you are peeling T-shirt over head, and that, *voilà!* you have a beautiful pair of breasts.

Final Scores of Doubleheader:

Arms 0, Breasts 2

Head 0, Breasts 2

8. Underwear Game

Pull underwear down. Place hands on buttocks. Voilà! Now you have a beautiful pair of breasts.

9. Being Wooed by Val

I was recovering from a bad breakup when the letters arrived. (My live-in boyfriend of two years had suddenly decided, after coming back from a five-day vacation in London, which he took by himself, that he must move to England. "I can't take this fascist country anymore," he declared, and left.)

The letters were pathetic and earnest. I had no idea who was sending them. I was amused, disgusted, and flattered. They were sent to the Roxy movie theater, where I was working as a ticket girl. The first one:

```
To love is to forgive each other.
Shouldn't we forgive each other?
```

Then:
```
The smallest defect is what endears
beloved to lover. I've seen your ring
finger. It saddens, yet haunts me.
```

Then:
```
To be the most articulate stutterer
in the world is my salutary aim.
Eloquence, that transvestite, cannot be
compared to the wobbliness I'm after,
the wobbliness of a heart disembodied—
propelled by lust and checked by
reason. I have a convoluted mind; I
have a saturated mind. I have a mind
that turns back on itself and eats
itself, like a twelve-headed snake
alternately kissing and swallowing,
only to have to defecate itself onto
the table every day while everyone is
watching. Shouldn't one be allowed an
occasional stump after decades of
hemorrhaging wildly at the drop of a
bucket?
```

Then:

> I apologize for the strangeness,
> even the offensiveness, of my last
> letter. I am approaching you this way
> only because of shyness. We are
> connected, I know. Will you join me in
> the house of light? Alone in my apart-
> ment, I can occasionally hear your
> thoughts. You love me. Last night you
> had a nightmare involving a car
> accident. Is that true?

I did lose two joints of my right ring finger in a minor car accident when I was eleven.

Then:

> I will come to the eight o'clock
> showing of *Sense and Sensibility* on
> Friday. You will recognize me immediately.
> But if, for whatever reason, reasonable or
> not, you choose not to acknowledge my
> presence, I will resign myself to that
> fact, and stop bothering you.

He gave me his name, in large block letters traced over several times:

> MY NAME IS VALENTINO

There was also a pencil drawing enclosed. "Nude and Skyhook" was scrawled in an ornate, tilted script across the bottom. Tucked into the top right corner was a spiderweb-like basketball net, its rim pointed downward. Running from bottom right corner to top left corner was a long drainpipe arm holding a marble-size basketball between its middle finger and thumb. The basketball had hair, eyelashes, growing on its circumference. The rest of the page was covered with a swirly pattern. There was no nude.

Because people tend to go to the movies in pairs, there are no more than ten loners at each showing. I assumed I was looking out for a single man, between twenty and forty. To make light of a bizarre situation, I kept saying, over and over, *Bulletproof glass, bulletproof glass.*

10. Sense and Sensibility

It was a Friday and I had a date with a girl I had just met. Her name was Patricia Potemkin. We were supposed to go the movies at eight o'clock. But I was sick that day and threw up several times during the afternoon. At five o'clock I took a nap and never woke up.

11. The Awakening

The Federal Water Conservation Act of 1978 mandated that newly installed toilets release no more than one and a half gallons per flush, 40 percent less than before. Many consumers complained that this only necessitated an additional flush.

Trish, however, applauded this new law. Why waste water? She was also keen on conserving electricity.

In 1979 a three-year-old Val ran into a darkened bathroom to pee, and saw, lying at the bottom of the toilet, a one-inch-long gold specimen, half broken up, diffused. "It's a ring," he thought. "What are you doing?" his mother said, startling him from behind. She was standing in the shower. Behind the translucent plastic curtain she looked like a pink octopus.

12. Gas Conservation

Trish was also keen on conserving gas. That's why the house was always ten degrees too cold and meals were routinely under-cooked. Chewy spaghetti, bleeding chicken, and rice that tasted like pebbles. Once, after Trish had placed a plate of warm baked beans with cold hot dogs in front of a by-now five-year-old Valentino, he said, "This tastes like shit, Mom."

"Just eat it."

"I can't, Mom."

"Just eat it!"

13. A Scat Singer

All through puberty I was afraid I would eat shit. Any day now, I thought, I would bend down over the toilet, pick some shit up, and eat it. What would I be if I ate shit? I would be lower than the lowest animal, you might as well shoot me. My two fears growing up were (1) I was going to stab myself with the bread knife while washing dishes, and (2) I was going to eat shit.

There is a word for this: *coprophagous,* meaning "feeding on dung" (dung beetle, etc.), from the Greek *kopros* ("dung"), derived from the Sanskrit *sakrt* ("dung"). *Kopros* in Greek means "dung," as in *acropolis:* "house of dung."

The only thing clean about a human being is his skin. Inside, he's filth. No, no, let's start all over: The only thing clean about a human being is his clothing. No! No! No! No! No! No! No! Because his pants and shirt are not clean. The only thing clean about a human being is his hat. And that, only on the outside. Everyone walks around with a load of shit.

14. A Recurring Dream

I dribble between my legs, behind my back, do a spin move, take off with da rock in one hand, pump twice in midair, and jam it down Michael Jordan's throat. "Fuck you, Mike! Fuck you!" His tongue is hanging out.

15. Bulletproof Glass

Four single men came to the eight o'clock showing of *Sense and Sensibility* that Friday:

• A short, red-haired man, in his mid-forties, with an unkempt mustache, tobacco-stained teeth, wearing a jean jacket.

"One, please."

"Uh, Val?"

"Just one, please."

• A very large, at least 230 pounds, black man, in his late twenties, wearing a Temple sweatshirt and a Phillies cap.

"One ticket, please."

"Valentino?"

"Huh?"

• A man in his sixties, in an old suit. Wisps of hair were sticking out of his ears.

• A dreadlocked, nose-ringed white man, in his early twenties, obviously drunk.

"One for *Sense and Sensibility*."

"Valentino?"

"Sense! Incense! Sissibilities!"

16. Destiny

What I said about the movie date was a lie. I did not know this girl. I had seen her just three times. She was a ticket girl at the Roxy movie theater on Sansom Street. I had written her a series of letters. I was in love. On that Friday I was supposed to show up to introduce myself.

The first time I saw her, I noticed, as she gave me my ticket, that the ring finger on her right hand was missing two joints! Blood rushed to my face. *It's providence,* I thought.

This fatal encounter triggered major chemical mayhem in me. I couldn't concentrate throughout the movie. All I could think of was this forlorn, brazen stump between her middle finger and her pinkie.

At home I would replay this scene over and over and imagine that my hand had actually brushed against her little stump. My life mission, from that point on, I knew, was to possess that stump.

A week later I went back to the Roxy. Although it was not very cold, I wore a ski mask. I saw her stump—again it made me shudder—and her name tag: Patricia Potemkin.

The third time I saw her, I was about to introduce myself, but I could not, I could not do it. I was too frightened to be confronted with destiny.

That's when I decided the best way to ingratiate myself into Patricia's life was through a clean medium. Through letters: words without breath, clean, dry, firm, minus the intangibles of a live body, with its corporeal garbage of seduction and repulsion.

17. Choice versus Bliss

But why was I so afraid of Patricia Potemkin?

Faced with an inevitable choice, a command dictated by fate, a man reserves the right to waver, to reject, even, what could be his ultimate happiness. Choice is dearer to him than bliss.

18. On Hair

You will concur with me that primitive people, people with low self-esteem, South Philly girls, for example, are the ones who pay the most attention to their hair. They like to braid, curl, conk, tease, weave, and dye their hair a hundred different colors. Those with a spiritual life, on the other hand, do not need to do this. They either pay no attention to their hair or go without hair altogether.

Starting from puberty, I had always been clean shaven: face, chest, armpits, crotch, everything. I even plucked my eyebrows and eyelashes. I would squat over a mirror and cut the hair sticking out of my ass.

It came as a complete surprise to me, then, that, during the weeks after my failure to appear at the Roxy for my so-called date, I had an irresistible urge to grow a beard.

19. Masked Man

A man wearing a ski mask approached the ticket window of the Roxy movie theater on Samson Street.

"Yes, can I help you?"

20. A Stump Devotee

It took me forever to corner Val into bed. No hints were too obvious. I'd lean over to pick up something in front of him wearing a loosefitting blouse with no bra underneath. I'd say, as we were sitting on his couch, "It's a little bit late, Val, I think I've missed my last train." Once I even gave him a tab of acid, his very first, but all he did was curled up in the fetal position in the bathtub and sob for three hours.

We did kiss, but his kisses were frantic, angry. He would pull my hair while he kissed me.

Finally I said, "Listen, Val, I'm not going home tonight. I'm not going home tonight."

We slept together for a week, he fully clothed and I naked. But he would not look at my body in the morning. Then one night, before bed, I got him to agree to strip to his underwear. I mounted him that night. "It's okay, it's okay," I hissed as I rode him up and down as he murmured. *From this point on,* I thought, *we will behave like a man and a woman.*

But why was I being so persistent?

It wasn't because I loved this man. I simply wanted to solve him. I wanted to give our relationship a definite shape before I walked away.

But still he was useless. You see, he couldn't maintain an erection inside my vagina. He could stay stiff for a long time as long as he didn't have to enter me.

And as long as he wasn't fellating my stump. Before, when we were just kissing, I noticed he had a habit of clutching my maimed hand, really squeezing it, and I had caught him staring at it few times, but now, now that he had lost his inhibition, it was all he wanted to do: give my stump a blow job. And after a couple minutes of that, nibble, nibble, nibble, he would pop and lose his erection.

I had had lovers who would make a point of acknowledging my stump during sex to show that they were not freaked out by it—true, some did seem to like it a little bit too much—but I had never met one who was this fascinated by it.

I realized the rest of me didn't exist as far as Val was concerned when I'd wake up, night after night, to find him fellating my stump.

21. The Index Finger

Like I said, maybe I shouldn't have named my son Valentino. But doesn't Valentino come from the Latin *valentia,* meaning "strength and valor"? Valentino = Valor = Valiant = Voluptuous = Vatic = Vast = Varied. It's strange how one word can determine the course of an entire life.

But it would be disingenuous of me if I didn't tell you about my index finger. It may have some relevance. I'm no shrink, of course, I'll just give you the facts:

I joined the National Guard in 1966. In 1968 I was called up to go to Vietnam. Now, the reason you joined the National Guard was to avoid going to Vietnam—so what was this bullshit? I was twenty-three, in love, and about to take over the family business—Buskin Hardware in Walla Walla. Why would I want to go to Vietnam?

But don't get the wrong impression. I'm no leftish tree-hugging faggot. If the Vietcong were to attack Portland tomorrow, I'd be the first to drive my Chevy down Route 12. But why would I go ten thousand miles to fight them in Saigon? For whom? For what?

In short, I was in a major crisis. What in hell was I going to do? I couldn't say anything to my own family. My father and two of his brothers were World War II vets. One came back with a plastic bladder. The only person who knew about my anxiety was Trish.

Each life is determined by two or three crucial moments. One night, after drinking a fifth of Jack, I went into the back of the store and flipped on the band saw. Its loud hum unnerved me for a moment, although it's a sound I've heard all my life. You can go for years on cruise control, but then, all of a sudden, you have to make a decision. And if you cannot do what is in your best interest, then you are a coward. No, worse, you are a pervert. Only a pervert shrinks from what is in his best interest. With my left hand I guided my right hand, its index finger sticking out, toward the blade. *Fluffffff!* That was it.

I felt no pain, only exhilaration. I was bleeding like hell, sure, but I was ecstatic. For the first time in my life I had made a decision that could not be reversed. I had taken charge of my destiny. I was a man.

You know how they always say, "It takes balls to do that!" It was literally true in this case: The second before my index finger hit the band saw, I felt a pinch in my testicles. They were blinking, so to speak. Gritting their teeth before their moment of truth.

But there was a logistical problem: I had made no provision for what to do after my amputation. With my bleeding stump pressed against the front of my flannel shirt, I walked back into the store and found a piece of cheesecloth, which I wrapped around my entire right hand. There was blood all over the floor and I thought, *Great, now I'll have to clean all of that shit up.* But the pain was starting to kick in, throbbing, increasing by the second and making me dizzy, and the cheesecloth had turned completely red. For a moment I thought I was going to bleed to death and die, right here, in Walla Walla.

Confronted with a novel crisis, the mind comes up with a novel solution. It was snowing outside. I went out, made sure I was not seen, knelt down on the ground, unwrapped my improvised bandage, and thrust my right hand into a mound of fresh snow. My blood coagulated.

My father never forgave me. He went to his grave thinking I had humiliated him.

I've never talked to Val about my index finger, and he has never asked me about it. I do not know if Trish ever said anything. Considering what he has done to his own body, it would not be appropriate to bring it up now.

Now that you've heard my little confession, tell me: What is the connection between a man cutting his trigger finger off because he did not want to get his balls blown off in a war he did not care about and a man hacking his penis off for no apparent reason during peacetime?

22. Lovers

I saw Patricia last month while waiting for the train in Trenton. It has been three years since we were lovers, two since my self-surgery.

I saw her out of the corner of my eye. She was leaning against a wall, standing about five feet away from me. Of course it was Patricia: still in her shades, black leather vest over white T-shirt, black leather pants, and black boots. I know this woman, I know her breasts and her vagina. I know her stump. Of course it was Patricia, with those thin lips. But I made no move to acknowledge her. I was in disguise. I was wearing a wig and a dress.

I stood still, looking up the track, while seeing Patricia out of the corner of my eye.

But I was not acting naturally. I neither turned my head left or right, nor shifted my weight from one foot to another. Nor blinked. Nor breathed. I stood perfectly still, like a classical statue, like the *Venus de Milo*, hoping that she would move so that I could move. But neither one of us moved. This went on for about two minutes. I knew then that she had recognized me. As the train came up the track, Patricia finally moved from her position and walked slowly but deliberately back into the station.

As I saw her from behind gliding up the escalator, I thought, *I know that woman, I know her vagina and her breasts.*

23. Patricia My Archivist

It was very unfortunate that Patricia saw me in my disguise. She had known me as a man, as her lover. There was no need for her to be devastated by my transformation.

More importantly, she was my archivist. She had known me during my happiest, most successful moments. If my life could be distilled to what was stored in her memories, then it would be considered a happy life.

It was a happy life, that is, until this episode in Trenton, this codicil, fucked it up. She had known me as a man with a beard, as her lover, as someone who gave her orgasms, not as a clean-shaven, dress-wearing faggot.

But if Patricia thinks I'm a faggot, then she's mistaken. I'm not a faggot. I'm not even a cross-dresser. It was a brief, misguided experiment. I wore dresses only for a few days.

What Patricia saw in Trenton was an hallucination, my hallucination. It was theater, a clumsy skit performed among friends, an amateur production, and not emblematic of anything. If you could walk into my job right now, you'd see a rather generic, tall, well-built, bearded gentleman in a conservative tie and suit, sitting at his cubicle.

24. A Flag with Wind

Aside from inspiring me to grow a beard, Patricia also inspired me to drink. It took the edge off our time together. It was also, as it is for everybody else, an aphrodisiac. It made me an enthusiastic lover. As a matter of fact, I don't think I ever penetrated her sober. Like the saying goes, a man without alcohol is like a flag without wind.

Unfortunately my drinking habit did not go away after Patricia and I split up. I drank and drank and drank and drank and drank. I drank and masturbated to revive our best moments together. The habit of shaving my entire body also came back. I shaved my face and my chest and my inguinal region. I plucked out my eyelashes and my eyebrows.

But I no longer had a spiritual foundation for these private rituals. I was a drunk who was compulsively depilating himself.

One night, as I was squatting over a small mirror to prune the hair from my ass, it happened.

I cut my dick off.

■ A Cultured Boy

I had to make him understand that there is a correspondence between touch and feeling, between gesture and emotion. I had to teach him that the body has a limited vocabulary, is a limited vocabulary, that there are only so many things we can do to each other.

Each touch must be warranted: an index finger on the lips, a head nestled between the breasts.

When it comes to physical contacts, to the dialogue between bodies, there is a hierarchy, absolute and vertical, corresponding to degrees of emotional intimacy. It is a gradation that must be sorted out and calibrated.

It was no small event when he placed his palm on my hip, when he rubbed his knuckles against my cheek. The first time his tongue entered my mouth, I thought his soul was trying to escape its solitary confinement to enter my body.

But he was impervious to the implications of these nuances. Later, when he fucked those girls, it was simply a kinetic spectacle, a punch up the middle, a twitch of the nerve.

He was my first. I chose him. We dated for seven weeks

before it happened. Our first date was at the Ritz. We saw *Remains of the Day*. We sat in The Last Drop and drank cappuccino. We took the 32 bus to the zoo on a Saturday afternoon. We went to the art museum on a Sunday. We gave each other books to read.

At the zoo we saw two massive turtles coupling: one tank teetering on top of another. He joked, "They look bored."

"You can't tell the male from the female," I said.

Later, back in my apartment, we sat on the couch, drank Rolling Rock, and read Walt Whitman out loud to each other. He thundered, *"What is this that frees me so in storms? What do my shouts amid lightnings and raging mean?"*

At midnight I said, "I think I'm ready for bed." He gave me an imploring look. We were drunk. He followed me to the door. We hugged. I gave him a kiss on the cheek. We had never touched lips. Impulsively I said, "Now for the other cheek." But before I could do this, kiss his other cheek, he intercepted my lips with his own. I had kissed boys before, but only perfunctorily, chastely, without passion. Never had one stuck his tongue into my mouth. He stuck his tongue into my mouth. I was shocked by its texture, by its violence. It was a thumb gyrating, a blind animal thrashing inside my face. I thought his soul was trying to escape its solitary confinement to enter my body. He kneaded my ass with his hands. He made these *um, um* sounds. He said, "You feel so good."

I pushed his chest away and said, "You'd better go."

How is it possible that, at nineteen, I had never really kissed a boy, never had sex? There is a correspondence between touch and feeling, between gesture and emotion. The body has a limited vocabulary, is a limited vocabulary. There are only so many things we can do to each other. Each touch must be warranted: an index finger on the lips, a head nestled between the breasts. When it comes to physical contacts, to the dialogue between bodies, there is a hierarchy, absolute and vertical, corresponding to degrees of emotional intimacy. It is a gradation that must be sorted out and calibrated. I had never fallen in love with anyone before Tom.

He was different. He was a cultured boy. At the museum he led me to Duchamp's *Étant donnés*. He could talk about any painter with authority. He said, "Fuck Raphael!" He recommended Duccio, Giotto, Masaccio, Morandi. He explained to me, with great lucidity, the parallels between Chinese painting, late Monet, and early Guston. He said, "Thomas Eakins had a chiffon fetish." He would rail against Jackson Pollock: "Yes, yes, yes, the artist pissing on the canvas.... What that guy represents, with his billboard canvases, repetition, and no content—unless you count acting out your adolescent sexual angst over and over, in the most jejune fashion, piss, piss, piss, as content—is America at its worst: smugness and megalomania fig-leafing a homicidal castration complex! And all that posturing: the painter as a sensitive athlete... a bald James Dean in jeans and T-shirt...."

His looks?

I never itemized his body. Never scrutinized it. I only had the most cursory awareness of his nose, his eyes, his shoulders, his forearms.... Physical attraction is a hindrance to love, I reasoned. One must get over it. Even in high school I'd become indignant whenever I heard a girl say, "That's guy's cute," or, "He's buff," or, "Nice buns."

Girls who talked that way were all about looks, were all visual strategists, were schemers. They preened themselves endlessly, farded their faces, and came up with subtle and not so subtle ways to highlight their tits and ass in order to create the necessary effects to lure as many boys as possible. They would say, "At the party I was standing by the onion dip surrounded by a herd of swains." They spent hours regarding themselves in reflective surfaces, the hood of a car, the pupils of your eyes as they're talking to you. Sexual display, always sexual display.

But love is not about looks because, within intimacy, the loved one's visual capital is quickly depleted, you can barely see him. If you're still staring at each other, then you are not intimates, because to stare is to acknowledge strangeness, novelty, even freakishness. It is a cruel and distancing act, what men indulge in at go-go bars. When you are in a new city, you stare, but at home you do not stare. That's why artists are the most alienated people, because they make a career out of staring. To become familiar, to become intimate, is to not see each other at all but to listen. The loved one is distilled to an instantly recognizable voice babbling endlessly.

Love is a communion of the minds, I thought, because the mind is the creator and repository of meanings. Unlike the body, the mind retains its elasticity through aging. It becomes increasingly more attractive, more profound, as the body collapses from within. You must anticipate, even look forward to, your lover's physical debasement, when there's no seduction left. When there's no bounce to his step, when he's groveling on the floor. Every physical attribute is random, unstable, a mere decoy, and has nothing to do with who someone really is. To say, for example, "He's five-ten, with chestnut hair, a hook nose," is to say nothing. *Hideous, handsome, radiant, striking* are all meaningless adjectives. The skin is cosmetic, a coat of paint: peel it off, burn it, and what's left is still the same person, and not just the same person but that person's essence. That's how you get to a person's essence, you burn his skin off. Any idiot can be seduced by a healthy body in the flush of youth, but to love someone is to envision cradling an invalid, or even a corpse, in your arms. It's the very emblem of love, cradling a corpse in your arms. The physical degradation of your lover is the first and last allegory. The body is merely a sem-aphoric armature to telegraph the soul's intentions.

He did not call me for three days after that kiss and I was relieved to be left alone. I needed time to think things over. I was scared of, yet eager for, what seemed inevitable. Finally the well-advertised, dreaded event. What are the means by which two clothed, talking people are transformed into sexual partners?

It was ten o'clock and I was in bed. I thought, *If he doesn't call me tomorrow, I will call him*. Then the phone rang. He said, "Susan, I'm across the street." His voice was fragile, cowed.

"What are you doing across the street?"

"I have a six-pack. We must talk."

"But I'm in bed."

"We must talk."

I opened the door to let him in. His meekness on the phone had emboldened me. He was a reduced person, discounted, remaindered. He was remaindered of the day. He even appeared shorter. Gone was the authority who could thunder, "El Greco sucks!" He had difficulties composing his face. I said, "Come, we can sit and talk on the bed."

He had only glimpsed my bedroom from the hallway while walking from the living room to the bathroom. He sat at the edge of the bed and observed his novel surroundings: a poster of a Georgia O'Keeffe painting; chrysanthemums in a carafe on my desk; well-stocked bookshelves. I was sitting on the bed with my legs crossed. He took out two bottles of Sam Adams from a paper bag and gave me one: "You have a bottle opening?"

"A bottle opener?"

"Oh, yes, ha! ha!"

"I don't think so."

"I'll open it with a key." He took out a set of keys and started to fumble with his own bottle, then he opened mine.

"Why are we drinking good beer? Any special reason?"

"No, no special occasion." He grinned. He had been studying my bookshelves as we were talking. "Robert Walser! When did you get that book?" He glided his hand over my knee, barely touching it.

"I bought it at Hibberd's a month ago for five bucks."

"Who told you about Walser?"

"No one."

He got up to pull the book from the shelf, then sat down again, but a little closer to me, a nearly imperceptible distance closer. He opened to a page: "Listen to this: *Perhaps because of a certain general weariness, I thought of a beautiful girl, and of how alone I was in the wide world, and that this could not be quite right.* Isn't that nice, the 'quite right'? He didn't say it was wrong; he said it 'could not be quite right' that he was alone. *Self-reproof touched me from behind my back and stood before me in my way, and I had to struggle hard.* Ha! ha!"

"Why is that funny?"

He did not answer but swigged his beer, then inched yet closer to me, a bald gesture, unprefaced by any statement. He sat perfectly still. We both sat perfectly still for a minute. He stood up unsteadily, in slow motion: "I've got to use the bathroom."

It's gluey, I'd been told, lots of glue. It's sticky like glue and even dries like glue. Elmer's Glue. When he came back, he had a panicky, sorrowful face and did not sit down: "Maybe I should go."

"Why?"

"I don't know."

You coward. "Then go."

"But I don't want to."

"Then sit down!"

He resumed his old spot, sitting sideways, bookward, with his face turned away from me. We both kept still for another minute. Then he turned to me and said, lugubriously, his eyes downcast, "It's great to see you."

I put my finger to his lips to spare him any more inanities. I turned the light off on the night table and pulled him closer to me. I whispered, "I want you."

I kissed him boldly, nibbling the corners of his mouth and his lower lip. I thrust my tongue inside. The mouth has no taste, only texture. I cradled his head with one hand and pushed him down onto the bed with the other. He slipped his hand under my T-shirt and fondled my breast. His palm was rough, calloused, and it made me shiver. He was slowly gaining on me, erasing my advantage. He took his shirt off, then his pants, then his underwear. I glanced at his shadowy crotch. It was a scumbled charcoal drawing, with the middle part lightly erased. He said, "Am I freaking you out?"

"I'm all right."

We continued. I was stung by his question. How did he know? When his hand slipped inside my panties, I began to tremble. My pelvis tried to wiggle away; it was thinking on its own. His hand was clamped to my crotch. My entire upper body began to convulse. It was a grotesque display, this loss of control: Now he's seen everything. He was about to pull my panties off, but I said, "No, Tom." I said, "No, please, don't." I steered his hand away in panic. He was touching me, down there. I was shaking violently. I was sobbing. Between sobs, I said, "I'm sorry."

"It's okay," he said, and kissed me on the forehead.

We slept. Or he slept and I pretended to sleep. I looked at his dark form and felt heat emanating from his back, from his asshole. In the middle of the night I peeled my panties off and pressed my body against his. He was lying on his side and turned away from me. (My body conformed to his.) I looped an arm around his torso, felt my breasts squished against his back. I could feel his ass.

The night was long. I touched myself, down there. I made myself wet.

At daybreak, as the blue light entered the room, I lifted the bedcover to peek at Tom, at this naked person. I had never seen a man naked.

Here was an eating/peeing/shitting body, nourished and exercised through two decades, a body at the pinnacle of its perfection, destined to be slashed, killed, corrupted, destined for ugliness. Here was a real human body, sleeping in my bed.

He was like a child. That's what a naked person is, a child. He opened his eyes and turned toward me. He smiled, brought his face close to mine. We kissed, but leisurely this time. He slid his face down, clamped his mouth around my nipples. First one, then the other. It's like eating. He squished my breasts together with his hands. Then he guided one of my hands toward his penis.

What is a penis? A silky stem, a paperweight, a pliable turd, an addendum. Something ancient, a dinosaur, a sage. It did not feel like it belonged on his body. Krazy Glued, it would snap right off with one hard yank. The head was shaped like the blade of a shovel, something to excavate with, or the reed of a saxophone. A downcast yet arrogant creature, defiant, dismal. Now I've touched a penis. I yanked it. I said, "Am I hurting you?" He laughed.

He rolled on top of me. His weight prevented my escape. I thought, *This is fucking. I'm being fucked.*

He lifted his torso to look down at our colliding pelvises. He wanted to register this unlikely act, to stash it away in memory. His soul was trying to escape from its solitary confinement. I heard the monotony of that swishy, swishy sound.

Afterward he lay draped over me, beached, his head nestled between my breasts. I asked, "Have you been with many people?"

Tom looked into my eyes, smiled, shook his head.

I stroked his black hair. He was twenty. I was nineteen. I had just been fucked.

I dressed quickly while he was in the bathroom. I did not want to be seen naked in daylight. When he came out, I was surprised to see that he was hard again.

He kissed me on the forehead before leaving. I had escorted him to the door. I was anxious to get rid of him. I wanted to be left alone to think about what had happened. I wanted him out of my apartment.

I went into the bedroom and took my clothes off.

I lay on the bed, uncovered. I opened my legs. I closed them. I kept them spread in a thirty-degree arc. I looked at the ceiling and saw his hovering face. I remembered the sucking, swishy, swishy sound. I remembered my fingers clenching his prick. *"Am I hurting you?"* Air and light played on my body. I became conscious of my toes and of my armpits.

I was an eating/peeing/shitting body, nourished and exercised through nineteen years, a body at the pinnacle of its perfection, destined to be slashed, killed, corrupted, destined for ugliness. I was a child, a naked woman. I had just been fucked.

Snatches of Tom's conversations, spanning two months,

droned in my head—"Everyone knows Bonnard as a colorist, unrivaled at painting cats, dogs, and buttocks, but they forget that he was also a great allegorist. His paintings are not just bouquets.... Miró's hovering assholes and cunts are traffic signs, devoid of sensuality.... Pollock is an inferior Monet"—and I thought, *Who gives a fuck!*

I did not go to class that morning. I thought, *If I go out, people will know.* I would give it away by how I walked, by how I smelled.

I caressed my thigh languorously, probed my insides. I stroked myself without shame, with brio, but then I felt bad afterward. It was a regression, this relapse. It was a parody. The term *post-masturbation* came into my mind. Already I was polluting the memory of my first fuck.

I closed my eyes and thought of our house in Swarthmore, of my father pulling weeds in the yard. He, too, has a prick. I thought of my mother. I was now her equal. There was nothing she knew that I did not know. When I woke up in the afternoon, I forgot, for a moment, that I had just been fucked.

I walked into the bathroom and stood in front of the full-length mirror. I looked at my breasts. He had seen these breasts. I looked at my pubic hair. He had seen this pubic hair. He had seen what I saw. I cupped my ass with my hands, dug my nails into its cheeks. I walked up to my astonished face and kissed the reflection of my lips.

As I brushed my teeth, I thought, *He has used this same toothbrush. We're sharing a toothbrush. Hygiene! That's what intimacy is: shared hygiene.*

The toilet seat was up. On the rim of the bowl was a long pubic hair: his pubic hair. *He has pissed into this bowl,* I thought, smiling. I showered quickly, got dressed and left the apartment.

It was very bright on the street. Trees, cars, and buildings all appeared in stark outlines, their colors saturated, fake-looking. Everything seemed made of plastic. It was a dressed-up yet degraded reality, a clutter of inconsequential objects, a charade of people scuttling about pretending to be doing things.

I strolled along with pleasure, with defiance, with hole, with happiness. The silk of my pants fluttered against my calves and ankles. I was astounded by the pliant workings of my insteps in locomotion. Yellow, fan-shaped gingko leaves flecked the sidewalk. I squashed the stinky peach-colored fruits under my mules. As I passed a bare-chested, sturdy-looking boy standing on a ladder, I tilted my face up and shouted, "Hi!"

I went to Rittenhouse Square and found a seat on the granite balustrade framing the reflecting pool, recessed from the flows of traffic in the dappled shade of the sycamores. There were many people in the square: mothers and nannies with their toddlers; aging white matrons accompanied by black nurses; paralegals, lawyers, and accountants in business attire going home from work; jeaned and T-shirted slackers. *Everyone has genitals,* I thought, *Let's not make too big a deal out of this.* I felt a part of this pantomime, initiated into the conspiracy of the universe. Silly phrases flooded my consciousness: *People must stick together…. She's stuck up…. If it's sticking up, hammer it down….A stick in the mud, he is…. I'm tired of your shtick….The weather's been sticky lately….I drive a stick shift, don't you?*

Nearby three boys of high school age, one with dreadlocks, were skateboarding. I looked at them with a knowing pleasure. I crossed, then recrossed my legs. I leaned back on my elbows, arched my back, pointed my nipples skyward. I felt giddy, let out a burst of laughter, which I tried to dissimulate as a coughing fit. A homeless man, picking through a trash can ten feet away, gave

me a drugged, hostile look. How unfair, I thought, that the homeless should go without sex.

He did not call me for two, three, four, five, six days. I thought,
It is okay. I'll give him time. It seemed perfectly natural that a man
should run away from a woman after a bout of intimacy. *Love
requires infinite patience,* I told myself. In any case I was swathed
in a glow of contentment and was not all that eager to have sex
again immediately. After a week I called him: "Tom?"

"Oh, hi! Susan!"

It was a little too breezy, this greeting, the emphasis on the
"hi!", the loudness of his voice. I half expected him to say, "May I
help you?" I said, "Tom, I haven't heard from you in a week."

"Well—ha!—I've been busy—ha! ha!—a few things came up
unexpectedly."

"What are you talking about?"

"Well, ah, can I call you back?"

I did not say anything.

"Susan, are you there?"

"Why are you acting like this?"

"Listen, are you going to be home tonight?" He had found
his voice. It was deeper, more serious.

"Why?"

"I can come by and we can talk."

"Let's meet somewhere else."

"Why can't we meet at your apartment?"

"Tom, what's up with you?"

"Nothing. Nothing's up with me."

"Meet me at Tangier."

"Tangier at Eighteenth and Lombard?"

"You know where it is. We've gone there together."

"All right. But when?"

"Eight o'clock."

"I'll see you then."

I went there half an hour early. I wanted to claim the space before he arrived. I also wanted to be drunk.

"Just one?" The waitress said after I had sat down at a table.

"For now."

"Would you like to see a menu?"

"No, thanks."

"What would you like to drink?"

"A snifter of Bailey's and a mug of Sam Adams."

Some guy at the bar in a yellow polo shirt glanced in my direction. He grinned. *What do you want, asshole?* I glowered at him and he looked away. Then I noticed the white spatters on his pants. It was the house painter I had said hello to on the street.

The music was loud. Some horrible free jazz. The waitress brought me my drinks. I drank the Bailey's in big gulps, holding the chocolaty liquid in my mouth for a few seconds before swallowing.

"Another Bailey's, please," I said to the waitress. "And, miss…" She turned around. "Is it possible to change this music?"

She hesitated, then said, "I'll tell the bartender."

"Thanks."

I thought it was important for us to meet in a civil environment, a public place where we would be surrounded by strangers, a deterrent to aberrant behavior.

The bartender switched to Chet Baker. *More crap,* I thought, *but at least it's soothing.*

Maybe he's afraid of being involved. Maybe he's gay. Maybe my body repulsed him. (It's true that my hips are a bit wide, my thighs a little too thick, but these imperfections are obvious through my clothes. Anyone can see them.) Maybe my pussy stinks. Maybe he's in love with somebody else, although I don't see how that's possible. Maybe he's offended by the way I escorted him out of the apartment.

The door opened. It was Tom.

"Hi, Susan."

"Hi, Tom." I had drunk four Bailey's and was feeling gentle, diffuse.

"Have you been here long?"

"I've just got here."

He sat down. The waitress came over. "Would you like to see a menu, sir?"

He looked at me. "Are we eating?"

"I'm not."

"Well, I'm eating."

The waitress handed him a menu. "Something to drink, sir?"

"A Hennessy, please."

He hid his face behind the menu until the waitress came back, then said, "I think I'll have the wings."

"Anything for you, miss?"

"Another Bailey's."

He reached across the table, grabbed my hand. I let him hold on to it. He said, "So! What have you been doing all week?"

"Masturbating."

"Ha! ha! Masturbating!" He looked toward the bar as if expecting the men there to laugh along with him. "Listen." He leaned his face forward, "I must tell you the truth. I've been seeing other people."

"What do you mean 'seeing other people'?"

He pulled his hand and face away, took a sip of the Hennessy, then leaned his face forward again. "You know: other women."

"What other women?"

"A bunch." He smiled. "I've been sleeping with them."

"Since when?"

"Since last week."

The waitress showed up with the wings. "Here you are, sir. Enjoy!"

He dunked a wing into the blue-cheese dipping sauce and started gnawing on it. He'd been fucking all week. He pushed the plate of wings toward me. "Help yourself."

"Tom, you told me you haven't been with many people."

"When did I say that?"

"After you screwed me."

"Did I actually say that?! I can't remember.... But if I did say it, then I was only telling the truth. You were only the third girl I've ever slept with. The first two were in high school. They were terrible! I had the worst sex. You were good. But this past week has been incredible. You've changed me, raised me to a new level." He smiled. "Thank you."

"Tom," I calmly said, "I thought we've been seeing each other."

"No," he said with surprising, firm malice, "we haven't been seeing each other. We've been talking to each other. You are a smart girl. I enjoy talking to you."

"Tom, why did you fuck me?"

"You fucked me!"

"I'm not joking, Tom. Why did you fuck me?"

"What's more important: talking or fucking?"

"That's not the question."

"Look, you're a smart girl. You're good-looking. What more can I say?"

He reached across the table, covered my hand with his. I pulled mine away. He rubbed the side of his foot back and forth against my ankle beneath the table. He said, "Susan, I'm sorry there's a misunderstanding between us, but why can't we just be friends? Why do we have to drag in all this emotional shit?"

"Do friends fuck each other?"

"If you can't fuck your friends, then who can you fuck?!"

He wiped the blue-cheese dripping from his lips, gnawed on another chicken wing. I said, "What about love?"

"Love! Love! Where do you see love?! It's a Greek chimera. They used to say 'I love you' before they buggered a little boy."

"Excuse me." I got up.

"Where are you going?" He grabbed me by the elbow.

"The bathroom."

I sat on the toilet. There was something ludicrous about my peeing, with my ass hovering above water and my vagina, a recent venue of so much drama, returned to its original function, a Narcissus contemplating itself. It is humiliating to be compared to, to have one's body compared to another. It is humiliating to have one's body compared to itself. He said that I was "good," and that the first two girls were "terrible." My naked body was an installment, one in a series. My breasts, rather large, with their brown, diffuse areolae, would now be seen in the light of other breasts, their relative merits carefully weighed and remarked upon.

He could, I suppose, if he wanted to, become a connoisseur of labial folds, of clitorises, and of ass hair.

He looked up from his plate of bones. "I thought you weren't coming back."

"Let's go."

"Where are we going?"

"Back to my apartment."

"Now?" His eyes sparkled. "But first let me pay for this."

"It's paid."

"See you later," the house painter said as we walked past him.

Outside it was cool, the first sign of autumn. I walked briskly, slightly ahead of him. He said, "What's the hurry?"

I laughed and broke into a sprint.

He ran after me. "You silly girl!"

As we waited for the light at the intersection of Nineteenth and South, a block away from my apartment, he clenched my shoulders, brought his face close to mine. I recognized his musk. It was our first kiss in a week.

"Wait, Tom." I pushed his chest away.

"You crazy slut!"

We entered my apartment like old lovers, a married couple returning from work. I did not flip on the light switch. We crossed the living room in darkness. "I've got to take a piss," he said.

He seemed relaxed, grateful. He was at home.

"I'll wait for you in the bedroom," I said. My father would flush the toilet to drown out the sound of his own pissing. Tom had no such modesty. I listened to the sound of his piss hitting water with frank lechery as I took my clothes off. I lay naked in bed and waited for sex.

As I watched him take his shirt and jeans off, watched him step out of his briefs, a tender grief welled up in me. Soon I would come to feel nostalgic over this naked body. He climbed into bed. That first touch along the length of our bodies was soothing. We kissed briefly.

"Tom."

"Yes, Susan."

"Will you kiss me down there?"

He understood. His face slithered halfway down my body, sank between my legs. He began by rubbing his nose against my hole. He lapped my vulva and nibbled the skin around it. For variety he kissed my ass. His face was working hard to convey its expressive range. It was competing against his prick. My vagina had become perceptive. He lapped and lapped and lapped. He was cleaning my toilet. It excited me that this mouth, which could talk so arrogantly about so many things, was smothered in my menstrual gorge, suckling my twat. I wanted to flush this face with urine, drench it with blood.

"Tom," I whispered.

"Yes, Susan."

"Stop."

He wanted to fuck, but I wouldn't let him. He asked me to jerk him off and I did. We slept. Or he slept and I pretended to sleep. I looked at his dark form and felt heat emanating from his back, from his asshole. In the middle of the night I got up and went to the kitchen. I opened the fridge and took out a can of Rolling Rock. I drank it staring out the kitchen window. The moon was a sliver of a smile in the starless sky.

When I left home for college, my mother had given me one of those Chinese meat cleavers. "It can cut anything," she said, "from carrot to chicken. The only thing it won't do is vacuum your floor." I had never really learned how to use this knife. I finished my beer and took it out of the drawer. To get the motion down, I hacked it through the air several times. I hacked it and hacked it and hacked it.

■ UNCLE TOM'S CABIN

Nineteen eighty-four was a very bad year for house painting. No one could get any work. By the middle of January, I was selling my books practically every day—hundreds of titles at a fraction of their original cost.

"Come on, Jay," I pleaded to the guy at the used-book store, "these books are out-of-print, man. Can't you give me a little bit more for them?"

"You know I always give you more for your books than I give anybody else," Jay replied. (And he was right, of course. I had taken my books to him for years, and he had always been very sympathetic.)

"You're just going to drink it all away at McGlinchey's anyway," Jay said as I walked out the door. One could buy a generic brand of baked beans, Hormel Chili, ground beef, or spaghetti and some jive sauce—the kind that is laced with sugar or even corn syrup—for two dollars or less, and a pint of Black and Tan at McGlinchey's was still less than a dollar.

Being broke and idle is a very bad combination if it drags

on for a while. I was going through old copies of *The New Yorker* looking for something new to read, jerking off, or paying for my beers at the bar with dimes and nickels. Whatever happened to all those losers I went to school with anyway? How come nobody's rich or famous? So what if Laura Humes hit the jackpot with the Daily Double! Big fuckin' deal!!!

Deborah Lansing, whom I hadn't seen for about two years, called around this time and left a message on my machine. I wasn't too keen on calling her back since she wasn't exactly friendly the last few times I had seen her on the street. It was rumored that the girl was on smack. Maybe she wanted to borrow money? I didn't have none, in any case. What else could she have wanted from me? Two more messages came, however, and I finally dialed her number.

"May I speak to Deborah, please," I asked when some old guy picked up the phone.

"May I ask who's calling?"

"Bui."

"Booey?!"

"Bui."

"Hold on a second."

Who's the geezer? I wondered, then Deborah's voice came on: "I'm so glad you called me back."

"How've you been?"

"Not good."

"What's the matter?"

"I can't really talk right now. Listen, can I stay at your place for a couple of days?"

I hesitated.

"It will only be for a couple of days," she continued, "I promise."

"When?"

"Tonight."

"Tonight?"

"It's sort of an emergency."

"All right. What time?"

"How about nine?"

"I'll see you then."

You just want her ass, a little voice told me as I hung up the phone. *But why shouldn't I think such thoughts? Because she's in trouble and she's asking for your help and you are incapable of helping anyone without tallying a potential benefit for yourself. Shut the fuck up, you righteous motherfucker. It's wrong, son, according to Our Lord Jesus Christ, Amen.* I hastily made a little sign of the cross in compliance. And just think, Deborah's dad is a retired USMC sergeant who did two tours in Nam to protect democracy for the likes of me....

Our first time was very forgettable. I was sitting at the bar, alone and lubricated, when she came in with two friends and sat down at a booth. *There's that Deborah,* I registered from behind my crazed lens, the cheery-looking one with a body like a pickup truck. "I like to sleep with Greg," she had told me on a previous occasion, "because he has such a big butt."

"You're like a monkey," she said to me later when we were totally fucked up and in bed.

"That makes me feel real good," I slurred after a pause.

"Don't be so sensitive," she said.

Another pause.

"Okay. You remind me of a squirrel."

"That's better," I said. Then we slept. There was a second time also, about a year later, and that, too, was very forgettable.

I will never, I had promised myself—*no matter how horny I get*—*sleep with this woman ever again.*

The stunted growth of my race, I've often reasoned, comes from the fact that we have, for the last forty centuries or so, eaten nothing but MSG, duck sauce, mung beans, hot mustard, fermented garbage, flakes of carrot, Ramen Pride, and an occasional glazed doughnut, to be washed down by cup after cup of the world's strongest coffee, sweetened by a digit or two of condensed milk at the bottom. *You were sired by a ring-tailed lemur,* goes a little ditty in my head, *and your mother is a gray squirrel!*

I imagined Deborah's father to be some boozy red-faced guy in a Phillies cap and an open shirt.

"Bui!"

"Yes, sir!"

"Do you know that I served two tours in your fuckin' country during the prime of my life?"

"Yes, sir!"

"Do you know that I risked getting myself killed by little bastards like you just to defend your fuckin' freedom?"

"Yes, sir."

"And you failed to satisfy my beautiful daughter?"

"I was drunk, sir!"

"I was drunk, too, when I fucked your mother twenty years ago!"

"You're a better man than I am, sir."

"You're damn right. I was in the United States Marines!"

I emptied a clip from my AK-47, bent down to retrieve the loose change from his pocket, doffed my V.C. helmet, and disappeared into the jungle.

Nine o'clock came and went and there was no sign of Deborah.

Around midnight, when I was already in bed but not yet asleep, the doorbell rang.

She came in, carrying two bags, looking flustered and apologetic. "Sorry I'm late."

"That's all right."

"I brought some beer."

I smiled.

"Were you sleeping?"

"I was lying down, yes."

"Can we drink in the bedroom?"

"Sure."

I could never recall her looking this haggard. She had a history of working one weird job after another, at the Rite Aid or something—when she was working at all—and the last time I had heard about her, she was going out with some drywaller from Port Richmond.

We stripped to our underwear and tucked ourselves quickly under the blankets. The heater in my apartment didn't put out very much, and it was extremely cold outside.

"This beer tastes good!" I exclaimed after downing the first can.

"It's Rolling Rock!" Deborah said.

"Anything is good if you haven't had it for a while."

"Are you broke?"

"I've been selling practically all my books," I gestured toward the nearly empty shelves. Deborah's features, even in the dim light, looked worn out and forlorn. *You are like a sister to me*, I mused, *we've known each other forever.*

"I'm down to ten bucks," she said as we both burst out laughing. I bent over the side of the bed to reach into the brown bag for another beer.

"Who's that guy who answered the phone this morning?"

"That's Walter."

"Who's Walter?"

"Walter's seventy-two."

"Seventy-two!"

"I've been staying with him."

"Why?"

"I was evicted from my apartment."

I pondered this information for a few seconds, then said, "Were you two, uh, lovers?"

"He would try to touch my butt when he passed by behind me, and every now and then he would try to kiss me."

"And that's all?"

"I wouldn't let him do anything else."

Deborah, I had noticed by this point, smelled unwashed, and there was a strong odor of tobacco issuing from her mouth. *How come,* I wondered, *some men get to sleep with virgins and I get to lie next to a bag lady?*

I opened another beer and wrapped my leg across her midsection, as I'm wont to do when I'm with someone.

"Let's turn off the light," Deborah said.

"Are you ready to sleep?"

"Soon."

"Okay."

"You mind if I take my bra off?" she said after the light was off.

"Go ahead."

We shifted positions a few times, found a comfortable

arrangement, lay still for a while, and said nothing. The three beers I'd had, on an empty stomach, were making me drowsy. *In a few weeks,* I thought, *the money will be coming in again, and this entire period will be but a bad memory.*

"You want to hear something funny?" Deborah said, breaking my train of thought.

"Tell me."

"But you must promise not to tell anyone."

"I won't."

"I almost became a prostitute!"

"No way," I said as I put a hand on her breast.

"I tried to get work at this escort service, but I was fired after only one day."

She turned her body sideways, nudged her nipples toward my face, and as I slipped my hand inside her panties, peeled her underwear off.

"I was sent to this hotel," she continued, "and I was really nervous, and this Japanese business guy answered the door, and he looked at me, and he slammed the door in my face!"

Her vagina was all dry, but she guided my hand back inside her as I tried to pull it away.

"That reminded me of something I read once," I said, "Have you ever heard of Arthur Koestler?"

"No," she answered, still arid.

"There's this story of him traveling through Azerbaijan. He was on a train, and the conductor opened the door to his compartment, and there was a peasant girl sitting there who wasn't supposed to be there, and the conductor was about to send the girl away when Koestler said, 'That's all right. She can stay.'" I paused at this point, propped myself up on an elbow, and took a swig from my fourth can of, by now, piss-warm Rolling Rock.

"Is that it?"

"No," I said, easing myself back down. "As soon as the conductor left them alone, the girl started to take off her blouse, and Koestler said, 'No, no, you don't have to do that,' and the girl got all pissed off and said, 'I'm sure the gentleman is used to finer ladies!'"

I let out a loud guffaw at this point, but Deborah did not laugh with me.

"And then what happened?"

"Nothing. The girl left the compartment because she was pissed off. Nothing happened." I glared at Deborah, a little annoyed. "The girl was a prostitute, get it? What Koestler thought was a simple peasant turned out to be a prostitute!"

Deborah rolled on top of me suddenly. "Bui," she said, "am I ugly?"

I hesitated, unwisely of course, but answered, "Of course you're not ugly."

I flipped her over so that I was now on top of her.

"Am I beautiful?" she asked, continuing her interrogation.

I hesitated, again unwisely, but said, "You're not ugly!"

"Of course I'm ugly," Deborah said. "That's why that Japanese guy slammed the door in my face!"

"You're not ugly," I said again, with more conviction this time, and gave her a full kiss on the mouth, which tasted, to my dismay, like an open can of Skoal chewing tobacco. "You're beautiful," I blurted. "You've always been beautiful." I was becoming delirious with my own momentum. "That Japanese guy is ugly. You're beautiful! Maybe he's used to finer ladies. Ha! ha!"

■ IN THE VEIN

I was hesitating in front of the Holiday Lounge, a place I had been a thousand times. I took out my cash and counted it again. Twenty-seven dollars—five cents a day for 540 days. I started to walk away but thought, *Fuck it,* turned around, and walked right into the Holiday Lounge.

I had forgotten how stale the air was, like tuberculosis, like the air on a Greyhound bus. Everything else was familiar: the drop ceiling like a vast Mondrian; the mural fragment of a waterfall, showing a pair of female legs dipping into a green pool; the Tiffany lamps dangling over the bar, with yellow tinsel garlanded between them; the portrait of a crying clown; the painting of a stag; the curving red-velvet wall, rubbed raw in spots, behind the small stage. I strode straight for the end of the bar and found myself a seat. There were maybe eight customers in the whole place: an old man in his late seventies, arthritic and trembling; two tittering Bolivians; a black queer on a recon mission....A chubby girl was dancing on stage. Norman was behind bar.

"Remember me?"

Norman squinted behind his bifocals. "Steve?"

"No, Tony."

"Did you move away?"

"I moved to Holmesburg, Norman, for eighteen months!"

"What did you do, mug somebody?"

"Possession."

Norman looked skeptical. "How long did you serve?"

"Eighteen months."

"Only eighteen months?"

The guy next to me leaned over: "Hey, I was in Nam for eleven months. I'd rather go to jail for eighteen months than go to Nam for even a fuckin' day."

The vet looked a little too young to be a Vietnam vet. His face was smooth, his eyes smiling. Maybe they had sent him in as the NVA tanks were rolling into Saigon. "Both of you guys are losers," Norman said. Then, to me, finally: "What would you like?"

"A Bud and a double Stoli."

The chubby girl wasn't so chubby after all. Her thighs were chubby but not her breasts. She had dyed-black hair, black lips, and black nails, a Gothic chick. Her bra and panties were still on and she was prancing around not doing much, someone you'd see at the beach. I tilted my Bud toward my lips but managed to miss them, spilling beer on my shirt. The vet laughed. "It's a two-dog night tonight. The other one ain't so hot either."

"She's all right," I said.

"No, she's not." The vet laughed.

The other one, a very tall blonde, was making her round collecting tips. She was wearing a countrified outfit, plaid top and bottom, all ranchy and homey. She had a kind, bewildered face, a face to wake up next to. She was rubbing her ass against the old man's knee. She wiggled and wiggled while Grandpa trembled, before saying coquettishly, "Stop digging!"

The vet whispered, "Whores, the whole lot of them."

Two days before I was released, Lady Di died. We were sitting in the day room watching it on TV, all seven of us except Fila Khiem, a Cambodian punk we called Pol Pot Belly, who was napping in his cell. Hank, a burly blond guy with a greasy goatee, a shit surgeon in a previous life, stood up and solemnly said, "The world has just lost a beloved slut, ladies and jism, but it will soon gain another one." Everyone burst out laughing. Mitch leaned his fat frame into me, slapped his tree-trunk thigh, and said, "Sheeiiiiit!"

"Give this jailbird a beer and a shot on me," the vet said to Norman.

We clanked bottles. The vet rolled up his shirt sleeves. "Check this out." I saw a slight, almost imperceptible discoloration of the skin on the inside of his right elbow. "Shrapnel," the vet explained. "You know, in many ways I'm glad I went to Nam. Once you've been shot at, once you know that your life can end—just like that!—before you even had a chance to do anything, there is this whole new other dimension to your life. Some experiences mark you as a—"

"Excuse me," I cut the vet short, "I have to make a phone call."

"Asshole," I muttered as I walked to the pay phone near the men's room to call my mother. "Mom?"

"Tony?"

"I'm out, Mom."

"You're out?!"

"I told you last week I'd be out on Tuesday."

"Jesus!"

"I'm in a bar having a beer."

She started to talk to someone else away from the phone.
I noticed the new pinball machine. Johnny Mnemonic: Meet the
Ultimate Hard Drive. Then: "You want to talk to Uncle Aaron?"

"Sure."

Uncle Aaron was my mother's boyfriend. They had been
going steady for about three years. "How you doin', Tone?"

"I'm okay, Uncle Aaron."

"Good to hear from you, very good to hear from you, kid.
Listen: I have a bottle of cognac here; we can shoot the shit later."

"Sounds good, Uncle Aaron."

"Listen: You know I've been diagnosed with prostate cancer?"
He already sounded plastered.

"Prostate cancer?"

"Yeah, just a month ago. Listen! You know what I'm saying?!
It's like this: The good Lord is always fuckin' with you, one way or
another; you go to jail for selling rocks, I have prostate cancer."

"I'm sorry, Uncle Aaron."

"You're sorry?! *I'm* so sorry. He fucks with you to wean you
away from all this bullshit, you know what I'm saying?"

"I've got to go, Uncle Aaron."

"And you want to know something else: your sister ran off
with a Chinaman!"

My mom came back on the phone: "It's all right, Tony. He's
a biker but only half Chinese. Adopted, I think. I'll tell you about
it when you get home."

I returned to my seat and saw that the tall blonde was dancing. She had stripped to her panties, baring tan lines and a pair of
pancake tits. Many more people had come in: two guys in business suits; an E-Z Park attendant; a house-painting crew… "This
one flashes," the vet advised. She was folded in half and leering

at me through her V-shaped legs. Then she flopped down onto her stomach, her ass sticking up and jiggling in a riding motion. This is what I must have looked like to them. "Three inches deep and all that power over us," the vet opined. "Five inches," I said. Meaning the asshole. Hankenstein jammed his big toe into me before he enlarged me with a razor. He inverted it into my slot and stroked up. Mitch was sitting on my back, holding me in a half nelson, while two guys, Timothy and Rufus, were sitting on my legs. She dimmed her eyes and stroked herself through her pink panties and, for a nanosecond, pulled the partition aside to give me a glimpse of what they were hallucinating. "She's winking at you, kid," the vet triumphantly said, as if he was responsible.

I drained my Bud. "How do you fit four faggots on a bar stool?"

"I don't know."

"You turn it upside down."

"Ha, ha, that's pretty good, 'you turn it upside down!' I got one for you: Why do women wear makeup and perfume?"

"Why?"

"Because they're ugly and they stink!"

I saw the vet's sallow face framed by mud, with shit in his mouth, shit in his eyes. "Do you know that in prison you lick your own spoon after every meal?"

"Whoa! Is this a joke?"

"Yeah! And one time this guy, Hankenstein, fucked me with my own spoon!"

It was past midnight when I left the Holiday Lounge. It had apparently rained hard while I was inside. Puddles pitted the street. My face felt tingly. I had to stop twice to throw up.

I took out my money and counted it. I had exactly $1.75

left, enough for bus fare plus 15 cents. The ride to my mother's house would take at least an hour.

At the bus stop there were only me and some pale kid, maybe twenty, with a red goatee. He was sporting a brown fedora and a muscle-T, to showcase at least a thousand dollars' worth of ink on his spindly arms. All kinds of bullshit: LA VIDA LOCO, a scorpion, a knife through the heart, a crying clown, four aces.... I looked left, then right, before walking up to him: "Yo, buddy, you got a cigarette?"

He gave me a Camel, but at arm's length.

"You got a light?"

He pulled out a Zippo lighter.

And this is exactly what happened next: As he came close, I grabbed the hair on both sides of his face, spat out my cigarette, and gave him a full kiss on the lips. He tried to scream, but I bit his nose, hard!, and would not let go until he slackened.

Then I let him go.

The sorry-assed faggot knelt on the ground for about a minute, wide-eyed and breathing through his mouth.

"Now," I blubbered, "can I kick you in the vein?"

■ Boo Hoo Hoo

Although Paradox lost his right contact lens in New Haven last night, he hasn't told anyone in the band about it. He is the road manager and owner of the van, a piece of junk he normally uses for his carpentry business—Paradox Home Improvements. Every time he switches lanes from left to right, he cuts somebody off. The last time, a Honda Civic started honking frantically, and Frank, riding shotgun, reached his beefy right arm out the window to flip off the driver, an older black woman. "Roll up the fuckin' window!" Karen yelled.

It is cold and drizzly, November weather. Karen is trying hard to fall asleep. Her head is tilted back, her cheek pressed against the windowpane. She has comically sad eyes on a cheerful face. When her eyes are closed, her face is happy. Karen plays a mean guitar. Slouched next to her on the middle seat is Tyler, the lead singer. The drummer, Orlando, lies awake in the back. Frank plays bass.

Paradox is hung over all over again. The blood vessels behind his eyeballs are being plucked by a determined hand. He is familiar with this ordeal, however, and is grimly enjoying it. As he drives, Paradox squints, bares his crooked teeth, and spits out phrases addressed to no one: "I'm sorry!" or "Unreal!" or "You're a fool!" He has driven the band so many times that they are well used to this behavior.

The sweet smell of bourbon seeping from the pores of Paradox's pasty skin is blending with all the other smells inside the van: a hard slice of cheese pizza lying facedown under the front seat; Frank's new leather jacket; Karen's perfume, sloshed into her armpits in place of the roll-on deodorant she forgot to bring.... They have been on the road for seven days, beginning in Philadelphia and stopping in Allentown, Scranton, Newark, Hartford, and New Haven.

Between them they know enough people to always have a place to crash after each gig. Last night they slept in Tyler's sister's living room. A single mother with a three-month-old baby, her apartment smelled like a cat's litter box. Right after coffee they took off. Now they are headed to Northampton, their last gig, then home. Almost broke, they skipped lunch this afternoon to save money.

The tour is not going too well. In Allentown they were paired with a speed metal band, Valhalla, and played in front of ten people. They have sold no T-shirts and only a few CDs. The highlights, so far, were Newark, where both Frank and Tyler got laid, and Hartford, where they were interviewed on a college radio station.

By the time they get to Northampton, everyone is exhausted. Tyler says, "Let's hope they'll give us some grub at this place." (In New Haven they were fed buffalo wings and given two pitchers of Iron City, while the headliners, Crucifux, were given entrees and salads. "We'll get that next year," Tyler said.)

"What's the name of the club?" Karen asks.

"Auto Da Fe," Paradox answers.

"Who we playing with?"

"Doctor At Tree."

Except for Paradox, forty and balding, the rest are in their late thirties. Veterans of many other bands, all unknown, they are already too old for this business. A breakthrough appears imminent, however: Their newly released CD has been reviewed in the *Village Voice* and *Spin*.

Even without tangible returns they would probably keep on playing anyway. At least until they're sixty. If you're a musician, that's what you do. What else is there?

If you sit back and think about it, of course it sucks to be in a band no one gives a shit about (and the majority of the people who do come to your shows are idiots anyway), but if you're a musician, that's what you do, even if you're too old for this business and they only pay you a hundred dollars a night, which, minus gas and divided by five, amounts to nothing.

But, all in all, they would rather be famous. Tyler always says, "When you're famous, people will cooperate with you. Fame is like a sexual musk. It entices the slaves to come out of the woodwork." He likes to quote Gertrude Stein: "What an artist needs most is praise."

Once he philosophized while tripping: "People think of fame as *temporal immortality* when in fact what it is is *spatial immortality*. You don't get to live forever but you do get to live everywhere at the same time."

Preening himself for eventual fame, Tyler has become hyperconscious of his appearance. He is nearly handsome, rugged, but with long, blond curls, which he likes to shake from side to side on stage. Once he tried shaving his head, thinking it would turn him into a skinhead or a convict. But a look in the mirror showed a buddha, if not a Chinese cook. He quickly grew his hair back. To get rid of his love handles, he has started to do sit-ups in the morning. There is a large tattoo of a ringing telephone on his right biceps, which he showcases by wearing a tank top whenever possible.

Paradox drives the van into the Auto Da Fe's nearly empty parking lot. "I'm sorry!" he shouts. The first thing they see inside is a mural of an orgy on the back wall. Swirling naked bodies in black, white, and yellow, with a slogan painted over it in red, white, and blue: MAKE LOVE NOT WAR BECAUSE WAR IS UGLY AND LOVE IS LOVELY.

The club has two large rooms: one with a long bar and one with a tiny stage. With the bad weather tonight they will be lucky to have fifty in the audience. The after-work crowd, who will be drunk and home by the time the music starts, sit at the bar and watch them lug in their gear. Some redheaded guy in a suit shouts "Hi!" to Karen. Two or three people laugh. The manager of Auto Da Fe, a very short guy with dyed-black hair, with a mouth set at an odd angle, in shades and a leather vest, comes out to greet them: "Doctor At Tree?"

"Sluice Gate," Tyler says.

Paradox approaches the little guy. He props his right hand in front of his own nose, slicing his face in half vertically. In a voice suddenly severe, he says, "I'm Paradox, the road manager."

"Nice to meet you, Pierre Docks. I'm Pablo."

"That's Tyler, Karen, Frank, and Orlando."

"Welcome. Welcome. Make yourself comfortable. The sound guy will be with you in a moment. We should have a nice crowd tonight. Drink as much as you want. Draft beer's on the house."

"How about food?" Paradox asks.

"We don't serve food here."

"How about bags of potato chips?" Paradox persists.

The manager turns to the bartender and says, "Give these guys some chips."

As they are doing their sound check, some drunk wanders over from the bar, huffing, and says to Frank, "What's the name of this band?" The drunk appears to be about fifty. He has an enormous red face, with a mouth that always hangs open.

It always annoys Frank when someone has to ask for the name of the band. If they were already in the club, then they should know. "Sluice Gate," he answers.

"That's about the dumbest name for a band I've ever heard," the drunk opines, then walks away.

"Who asked for your fuckin' opinion!" Frank yells after him.

After sound check, Orlando, Tyler, and Karen go back to the van to smoke a joint. Paradox and Frank stay behind at the bar. There is Sam Adams on tap and each has a mug in front of him.

"You know, I'm sort of from this area." Frank grins.

Paradox squints for a long time, then shouts, "Smooth bore!"

Inside the van Karen, mellowed by pot, lies on her side on the backseat with her eyes closed. Although not altogether beautiful, she has a face that will never be scored by experiences, that will never grow old. It will stay young, one suspects, even inside a coffin. "Look," Tyler says, "they misspelled the name of our band on this flyer."

"Let's see," Orlando reaches for the flyer. "Sluice Gait," it says.

"I kind of like this version," Orlando concludes. "It says here that the Nguyens are playing here tomorrow."

"Put some music on," Karen says.

Tyler shoves a cassette into the tape deck.

"Who's this?" Karen asks.

"Blind Lemon Jefferson."

"Sounds good. I've never heard of him!"

Tyler takes a long drag, then says: "You know, this guy died walking into a snowstorm after a recording session."

"Was he on drugs?"

"No. Blind!"

"I get it: Blind Melon!"

"That's where they got their name."

"You know everything!"

The van has become a bubble of mellowness. After a moment Karen says, with her eyes still closed, "You know why semen tastes kinda sweet?"

"I wouldn't know," Tyler says. "Why does semen taste kinda sweet, Orlando?"

Orlando is gay and was once the drummer for Pansy Division.

"Because of beer," Karen answers.

The door to the bar opens and the drunk comes out. He walks over to a pay phone but does not make a call. He stands at the pay phone for a while, in the shadow, with his back to the street. When he has finished and is returning to the bar, he sees the van. He recognizes Tyler, smiles, and mouths the words "fuck you." Then he goes back inside.

"What was that all about?" Orlando says.

"Why? What happened?" Karen asks.

"Some guy just said 'fuck you' to Tyler."

"This is a lovely town," Tyler says. They all laugh.

Girls from Smith and Amherst are showing their IDs to the bouncer at the door. The jukebox is blaring Nirvana. Frank downs two double shots of Southern Comfort in quick succession. A fat girl walks up to him. "Excuse me," she lisps, "are you the guitarist for Doctor At Tree?"

"Yes, I am."

"I love your CD."

"Thanks."

"Would you sign this flyer for me?"

"Sure."

She gives Frank a pen.

"What's your name?"

"Susan."

Frank turns to Paradox and whispers: "What's the name of the guitarist for Doctor At Tree?"

"How the fuck do I know?!"

To Susan. Love, How the Fuck Do I Know, he scrawls in a loopy script.

After the fat girl goes away, Paradox comments, "Nice-looking girl."

"You fuck her," Frank says.

Five minutes before they are to go on, Frank's mother shows up. She has groceries for the band. White bread, salami, cheese, and apples. "Thanks, Mrs. Johnston," Tyler smiles. Frank pulls her aside: "What do you think you're doing, Mom?"

"I just came by to say hello."

"But I'm a rock musician, Mother!"

"Do you need money?"

Frank doesn't answer. Mrs. Johnston stuffs eighty dollars into her son's shirt pocket, then leaves.

They begin with "Sucker Punch," "Sweet and Sour Sue," and "Sweeny Erect." Tyler writes most of their lyrics. *Spin* has called him a poet. For "Sweeny Erect," he jumbles fragments from Eliot into an incoherent whole. On another song, "Hyacinth Girl," he takes a section of "The Waste Land" and sings the lines in reverse order:

> *"Looking into the heart of light, the silence.*
> *Living nor death, and I knew nothing,*
> *Speak, and my eyes failed, I was neither*
> *Your arms full, and your hair wet, I could not…"*

They play inspired. The crowd, mostly there for Doctor At Tree, drift in and out of the room.

Paradox is still sitting at the bar, downing shots of Turkey. There is a girl sitting next to him. To make conversation, she says, "Do you like Sylvia Plath?" She has long eyelashes and wears purple lipstick. Her breath smells like Stoli. "Unreal!" Paradox shouts. Then "You're a fool!" Then "I'm sorry!"

Just before midnight the band finishes with a ska version of the Strapping Fieldhands' "Boo Hoo Hoo": *Boo hoo hoo! I'm in love with you! Boo hoo hoo! Boo hoo hoo!* Tyler is wailing, his head swiveling like a gift-shop doll's. He turns and sees Karen smiling at him. They were lovers once. Many have tried, including Frank. "Boo hoo hoo! Boo hoo hoo!" The thin crowd applauds. They pack up quickly, then leave.

Tyler, Karen, and Orlando are sleeping quietly. Although the trees are very beautiful this time of year, you can't see them in the dark. They are heading south on Interstate 91.

"How many more hours to Boston?" Frank asks.

"Less than two," Paradox answers.

"Is that all?"

"That's all."

Outside Holyoke it finally happens. Reading from a sign overhead, Paradox shouts, "Dinosaur footprints!" The driver of the Lexus sees the van veer into his lane but cannot do anything about it. It sounds like an explosion.

Just before the moment of impact Tyler dreamed he was sitting in an airplane while dinner was being served. Karen was the stewardess. She asked him, "Beef or chicken for you, sir?"

"Both!" he answered.

"Holy fuck!" someone screamed.

Mortified by his snafu, Tyler tried to mouth the word *chicken* but, again, he could only say "both!"

The van flipped four or five times before bursting into flames. It had knocked out three cars going in the opposite direction. Karen's head was tilted back, her cheek pressed against the windowpane.

■ 555

The pack of 555 was a sure giveaway.

"Give that guy a shot on me, Fergie," I said, gesturing toward the scowling man sitting by the cash register, a pack of 555 in front of him. It was a Saturday afternoon, in the summer, and most of the ten people sitting at the bar had their faces tilted toward the TV. Lenny Dykstra, going against Maddux, was working the count to 2 and 2. There was no score in the third. The bases were empty.

In fifteen years of going to McGlinchey's, this was only the third or fourth time I had seen a Vietnamese there. Koreans and Chinese, yes, but almost never a Vietnamese. I walked down the length of the bar and sat next to him. I began, in Vietnamese: "I'm Bui."

"I'm Thanh."

"First time here?"

"Yeah."

"The drinks are cheap in this place."

"It's not an issue," the man replied, somewhat oddly. He

was about forty-five, brown-skinned, sturdy-looking, with a perpetual squint in his eyes, betraying a catatonic form of concentration.

"Want a shot?" I asked.

"Sure."

"What do you drink?"

"It makes no difference."

"What was that you just had?" I pointed to the empty shot glass in front of him.

"I don't know."

"Then how did you order it?"

"I pointed to that old guy across the bar and said: 'Shame!'"

"Two Jamesons, Fergie."

Thanh looked at me, squinting. "How long have you been in America?"

"Since I was eleven," I said, "since 1975. How about you?"

"Seven months."

"Seven months!"

"Look," he opened his mouth wide, "I got no front teeth." And he really didn't.

"What happened?"

"Prison."

"They rotted?"

"No, punched out!"

"V.C.?"

"V.C."

I felt elation, then shame. To chase this feeling away, I offered, "Two more shots?"

"I'll buy this time," Thanh countered.

"Two more, Fergie."

I thought of a man I had met once who, after the war, was imprisoned for thirteen months in a tiny underground cubicle. He used the cotton lining from his flak jacket to wipe his ass. When Fergie came back, Thanh gave him a five-dollar tip.

"That's too much," I whispered as the bartender walked away.

"Money is not an issue when I'm out partying," Thanh sternly said. He snuffed out his cigarette, then lit up another 555. He handed me a dollar. "Could you put music on the jukebox?"

"Any preference?"

"Doesn't matter."

I went to the jukebox and punched in Nina Simone, Patsy Cline, Sam Cooke, and Dylan, bypassing the grunge. When I came back, my friend said, "I came to town today to fuck a whore."

"What?"

"Fuck a whore in Chinatown."

"Oh."

"There's a massage parlor at Eleventh and Arch. You pay forty dollars for a massage, then twenty dollars for a blow job, or fifty dollars for a lube job."

"A what?"

"A lube job. You've been away from Vietnam too long."

I had once paid a red-headed girl in Washington. "So how was it today?"

"I didn't fuck her. The girl I picked was Vietnamese, but I didn't know it at first."

"The girls are usually not Vietnamese?"

"No, they are all Koreans. Some of them are Chinese, but never a Vietnamese.

"I've been going there every other payday—once a month,

for about five months. The girls there are not so pretty, but they are pleasant, and the place is clean."

The place is clean and the girls are pleasant. You find it by word of mouth. It is on a second and third floor, over a travel agency with posters of Hong Kong, Seoul, and Ho Chi Minh City in the plate-glass window. Next door is a Cantonese restaurant serving dim sum on Sundays. At street level, above a dirty glass door, is a tiny red sign with a single Chinese character for *Gym*. There is nothing to see beyond this glass door but the green-carpeted stairway. A surveillance camera browbeats you from its stanchion. You ring the doorbell, wait for the Korean bouncer to buzz you in.

Thanh sat on the green couch, fidgeting with his complimentary midget-size can of Coke. It was noon outside, but inside, with the windows painted over, it was always evening. Three nearly naked girls, returning from their assignments upstairs, were arrayed on a row of folding chairs against the opposite wall. One of them had to stifle yawns. Up all night, they were waiting for another hour so that they could go home. The burly Korean bouncer, with a quarter in his left ear, chewing on a toothpick, was sitting at his desk meticulously cleaning a .22. Thanh was not satisfied with the current selection, and neither were the other two customers. On the couch with Thanh was a cook from Ho Sai Gai, in his white uniform, yellowed by old grease. To his right was a baby-faced guy, not bad looking, about twenty-two, sitting on an easy chair. He didn't lean back but was hunched forward, with his forearms resting on his thighs. He was sniffling and wiping his nose periodically with the back of a hand. He stank of beer. *Why,* Thanh thought, *would a kid like this go to a whorehouse and pay almost a hundred bucks to get laid? Can't he find a girlfriend? A* new girl entered the room: short, small-breasted, with a cheery, innocent face, wearing a green silk blouse. She smiled. As the cook and the baby-faced guy hesitated, Thanh stood up, nodded at the girl, and walked to the desk. He forked over his forty dollars, took his sneakers off, and followed her upstairs. She led him down a corridor, stopping at a linen closet to pick up a white towel. The fact that these transactions were often carried out with little or no conversation suited him perfectly. He never picked the same girl twice. The idea of fucking a complete stranger appealed to him morally. No dissimulation—that's what he liked about it— only intimacy.

The room had a queen-sized bed and a chair, to put your clothes on. It was lit by a single red bulb. There was a shower stall, but no toilet. Thanh promptly took his T-shirt off, stepped out of his jeans, and walked into the shower. The girl stuck a hand under the jets of hot water, fidgeting with the knobs. It was a bit too hot, but he said nothing. Still in her blouse and panties, she stood to the side and ran a new bar of soap all over his wet body. Then she rubbed him with a big sponge, lingering for a long time about his privates. Although her movements were efficient and perfunctory, like a man washing his car, or a mother her child, he was genuinely touched by this attention. He watched her small, bent figure, and thought of an incident from the night before: Someone had thrown an egg at him from a passing car. It landed at his feet, spattering his sneakers with yolk. He saw a blond girl in the passenger's window. She was yelling something.

The water was turned off and she dried him with the towel. She held his hand and walked him to the bed. "I must sleep," she said, "I've been up all night. I must sleep for five minutes, then we can fuck."

She lay down on her stomach, closed her eyes, her face turned away from him. Thanh, erect, lay next to her. He wanted to sniff her hair but dared not. He stared at her white panties, pink in that light, for a moment before deciding to peel them off. She yanked them back on. "My ass is cold!"

"*Du Me!*" he cursed.

The girl turned around, frowning. "You're Vietnamese!" she said in Vietnamese.

"And so are you."

He grabbed the towel to cover his prick, which had suddenly gone limp.

"What's your name, Brother?"

"Thanh."

"Nice to meet you, Brother Thanh."

"And your name?"

"Huong."

"Your real name?"

"That is my real name."

They laughed. Her face brightened up.

"How old are you, Huong?"

"Why should I tell you?"

Huong looked about seventeen. Thanh said, "Are you in school?"

Huong nodded.

"What are you doing in a place like this?"

"What do you think?"

"You should be home studying."

Huong stared at Thanh, expressionless. In two quick motions she pulled her blouse and panties off. "Let's get this over with," she said. "I've got to go home."

Thanh did not move, the white towel still covering his prick. "What do you study at school?"

Huong, becoming irritated, said, "Five more minutes and I'm going back downstairs."

"I don't want to, uh, fuck anymore," Thanh said, "but I'll pay you for your time."

Huong cheered up. "I study history, biology, English, and French."

"Conjugate the verb *être* for me."

"You must think I'm stupid."

"I'll give you fifty more bucks if you can conjugate *être* for me."

Huong's lips were pressed together in consternation. She thought it over, then said, "I'll conjugate *être* if you promise never to come here on the weekend again."

"Why?"

"Because I'll never want to see you again."

"It's a deal."

"*Je suis,*" Huong blurted, with vehemence, accenting each syllable, "*Tu es. Il est. Elle est. Nous sommes. Vous êtes. Ils sont. Elles sont.*"

■ TWO WHO FORGOT

There is no reliable method of calibrating degrees of suffering, and of the countless mishaps and irritations a passenger may encounter while riding the train from Hanoi to Saigon, I will only catalog a small inventory. A breakdown of the kinds of explosives and bombs that were used to destroy its 1,334 bridges, 27 tunnels, 158 stations, and 1,370 switches during the Vietnam War would be useless and incomprehensible. I do know that the poet Do Kh, traveling in 1992, fell asleep during the stretch between Ha Tinh and Vinh while trying to read Duong Thu Huong's *Love Stories Told Before Dawn*. And in Bao Ninh's uneven novel, *The Sorrow of War*, there is an extraordinary account of the protagonist and his girlfriend, recently raped during the confusion of a bombing raid, walking away from the wreckage of their train in tatters, only to be approached by an old beggar soliciting alms. And Tran Huynh Chau, a former ARVN officer, tells in his memoir of nearly being hit by a rock pitched through the window as his train passed through Nha Trang, a resort town renowned for its beaches, snorkeling, and scuba diving. It was 1980 and he was heading home after five years in prison. The 960 miles from Thanh Hoa to Saigon would take sixty hours. Each prisoner was given fifty dong as he was released, a kind of severance pay; Chau's ticket cost forty-five. The custom of hurling rocks at trains began after the war when children in the South decided to take aim at the pith-helmeted heads of the Northern soldiers sitting inside train windows.

A couple of train-related incidents occurred during the early hours and late afternoon of June 3, 1995, but before we get to the details, I must give you some background information on what I was doing in Vietnam in the first place. On May 3, 1995, at the age of thirty-one and after an absence of twenty years, I returned from Philadelphia to Vietnam, the country of my birth, for a one-month stay. I had left Saigon on April 27, 1975, sitting on the floor in the hold of a C-130 cargo plane, a few hours before NVA rockets shut down the runways of Tan Son Nhat Airport.

Returning in a Boeing 747, my reentry into Vietnam's airspace was lubricated by the sweet voice of Blossom Dearie, one of the many inspired selections on the jazz channel of Vietnam Airlines. Below, and a little to the right, was the red earth of the central plains, patched by swaths of emerald-green rice fields and hemmed on one side by the turquoise-blue of the Pacific Ocean. The Suntori whiskey I had drunk at Seoul's Kempo Airport was starting to kick in, and I imagined myself to be greatly moved by the occasion. Alcohol, which always makes me either maudlin or violent, was the likely culprit for my agitated state. It is, again, last call at Dirty Frank's—a bar I frequent in Philadelphia, where Blossom Dearie is also available, on the jukebox—and I hear the bartender's raspy voice telling me to go home. "I'm going home, Al. I'm going home."

Although Saigon-born and raised, I had decided early on to spend the bulk of my time in the northern part of the country, since both of my parents are from the North (my spoken Vietnamese, to this day, betrays this genesis). During my stay in Hanoi, Hai Phong, Thai Binh, and elsewhere, I was seldom mistaken for a local, and often assumed to be a Chinese, a Japanese, or a Korean. I was even called Ong Tay, literally "Mr. West," a Westerner, a word that used to denote only a Frenchman. A practical consequence of this fact was that I was always seen as a foreigner and was always charged accordingly for my accommodations. I should point out that an overseas Vietnamese was also considered a foreigner, but if one looked a certain way, one could occasionally pass as an ordinary Vietnamese.

I did not look like an ordinary Vietnamese. Although a small man in America, I was deemed fat in Vietnam, with a belly well-stoked by case after case of Rolling Rock, the well-known Pennsylvania brew. On top of this I sported a goatee and a crew cut, two conceits seldom seen on Vietnamese men, who prefer to keep their face either clean shaven or with a small, well-trimmed mustache, and their straight hair like a mop of grass.

When it was time for me to buy a rail ticket for my trip from Hanoi to Saigon, I was willing to pay the foreign price. Any thought I had of presenting myself as a local and saving a hundred bucks was further discouraged by a story I'd heard of an overseas Vietnamese who'd managed to buy a cheaper ticket, only to be docked the difference while on the train, as he had sprinkled his Vietnamese conversation with one too many *okays*, thus revealing himself to be an outsider.

"Sister, give me a first-class ticket to Saigon," I said to the lady behind the booth.

"Four hundred ninety thousand dong," she told me.

I hesitated, knowing the quoted price was too low: "Sister, give me the foreign price."

She looked at my face more carefully: "One million four hundred ninety thousand dong."

I gave her the money. She continued: "You speak like a local."

"My mother is from Hanoi."

"Traveling alone, Brother?"

"Yes."

"Fancy luggage?"

"No."

"Why don't you pay the cheaper price?"

I will have to pay this sly broad ten bucks for the transaction, I thought. Not a bad deal. I said, "If you think I can get away with it, Sister, then give me the cheaper ticket."

She gave me back my change, with the ten bucks already deleted.

I was half suspecting the ticket agent to have pulled a quick one on me, for even if I was penalized on the train, she'd still get to keep her ten dollars. Whatever the case may have been, the next task for me was to disguise myself accordingly: In conformity with local taste, I shaved off my goatee, bought off the street a 60-cent hat with "Noontime Lover" (in English) stenciled on it, and a $2.50 yellow shirt (bargained down from $4.00), waited for departure date, and hoped I wouldn't be detected on the train. I decided against buying a pith helmet—worn by Communist troops during the war but common among civilians throughout the North—not because of politics but because I thought such an attempt at a makeover to overshoot the mark; truth is, many Hanoians, taking their fashion cues from imported videos produced in Orange County, California, were going the other way, trying to look like Vietnamese-Americans.

"Buy earplugs," an American friend advised, "because of the deafening noise." A few others told me to bring along my own food since the meals on board were inedible. I went out and bought canned pâté, peanuts, a bottle of La Vie spring water, and boxes of La Vache Qui Rit, or Laughing Cow, an imported, buttery processed cheese, ubiquitous throughout the country, even in the most remote provinces. Petty thievery would not be a problem, since I would be sharing a cubicle with only one other person.

The reason for going through all the hassles of traveling by train, instead of by plane, was that I wanted to see the countryside. Never before a picture taker, I had suddenly developed the passion in Vietnam and was hoping to take a few good shots while on the train. Before I left the States, an aunt had lent me her camera, which I grudgingly accepted. "Take a few shots," she said. "It is your country." (This aunt also warned me against mosquito bites. "They like our flesh better than the locals'," she said. "We have more protein in our blood." I was incredulous: "How can they tell?!" "They can smell it.") Once I got to Vietnam, the impulse to take pictures—an impulse I had previously despised in other people—took over. Everywhere I went, I took shots of people going about their business: the Black Thai, White Thai, Kha Mu, Meo, and Muong peoples I encountered on the road from Dien Bien Phu to Sapa; a wiry old guy, in a faded army shirt and shorts, carrying a red chicken in a rattan cage, who snapped to attention with a military salute as I aimed my Canon at him ("I'll send you a copy," I promised); karaoke-bar hostesses; pool players; working people drinking. I fancied myself to be no tourist, no ordinary picture snapper, but a spy, an infiltrator, capable of delving beneath the surface of things. With an irrepressible pleasure, I anticipated the moment of my return to the United States, when I could develop my twenty rolls of film.

The resumption of the Hanoi-Saigon Line, dubbed the "Unification Line," on September 31, 1976, twenty months after the fall of Saigon, was a symbolic achievement and a source of great pride for the Hanoi regime. I entered a small cubicle, laid down my meager luggage, and sat on the lower berth to study an environment that would be my home for the next thirty-six hours: an oscillating fan bolted onto the ceiling; a small sink inside a cabinet; a table that folded into the wall; wire mesh in the window—a visual hindrance as far as the views were concerned. A very old man, my traveling companion, walked in, and it took me a few seconds to realize that I should yield him my lower berth since he was obviously in no shape to climb up and down from the upper one. The old guy appreciated the gesture. He took out from his blue vinyl bag a one-gallon Coke bottle filled with a homemade rice wine, and poured its content into two teacups, which we quickly emptied. For the duration of the trip the bottle was constantly out, and each time, except for the one instance I wish I could undo now, he managed to outdrink me.

"We're both wine people," he barked. "Be natural!"

"Thank you, Uncle," I replied. "I'm lucky to meet you."

"Be natural! Be perfectly natural!"

The old man was a Hanoi native, he told me. "Are you a Saigonese?"

"Yes, I live near An Dong Market." (It's my grandmother's address.)

"I first saw Saigon in 1975. I liked it so much, I stayed." He chuckled. Now he went back and forth on the train several times a year, he said. To endure these long trips, he must be drunk from beginning to end.

"Not a bad idea," I told him.

"But you know something?" He stared and leaned into me, his red eyes lit up. "I'm always drunk anyway, whether I'm on the train or not!"

I could have told him how I was also a twenty-four-hour drunk in Philadelphia. How, during an average week, I would go to maybe five different bars, sometimes five different bars in a single night. How drinking in America is often a solitary exercise, even if it's done in public.

There is an after-hours club, the Pen & Pencil on Sansom Street, where you can drink until five in the morning and watch the pale orange light of dawn slowly illuminate its bay window.

When the train finally rumbled out of the station, I was immediately sorry I had forgotten to buy a set of earplugs, for, with rarely a letup, the old train made a racket equivalent to any industrial-noise band (Sink Manhattan, for example, or Missing Foundation). The food, on the other hand, did not turn out to be half bad—stewed pork over rice, roasted pork with rice noodles in broth, bananas for dessert—and I managed to eat what was given me, supplementing my meals occasionally with a wedge of Laughing Cow.

While the old man slept, I stared out the window. All views were obstructed by the rusty screen: the gold glare of the tropical sun, men standing in mud, a white heron shaving the green stalks of the rice paddies.... I took photographs of the cubicle, of the old man's stiff body sleeping, of the oscillating fan. I took photographs of the vendors selling magazines and cans of soda at the stations, of the civic posters hectoring the populace to improve their public behavior. I took photographs of the squatting toilet on the train, which I thought were among my best photographs.

Vinh. Dong Hoi. Dong Ha. Sink Manhattan. Sink Manhattan. Sink Manhattan. Hue. Da Nang. Quang Ngai. Sink Manhattan. Sink Manhattan. Sink Manhattan. Dieu Tri. Tuy Hoa. Nha Trang. Sink Manhattan. Sink Manhattan. Sink Manhattan. The cities ticked by, hives of humanity, old sites of battles, mortared, bombed no longer.

In spite of the deafening noise, I had to lie down. What an exhausting month it had been. Before this trip I had found myself in a particularly cantankerous mood in Philadelphia, and always, it seemed, on the verge of an altercation. "Stay anywhere long enough," Céline wrote, "and the people around you will start to stink up just for your special benefit." After Vietnam, however, Philadelphia will be possible again. One goes away merely to distract oneself from the complexities of home. On my first night in Vietnam, as I was walking on Hung Vuong Boulevard—literally, since there was no room on the sidewalk—disoriented by the motorcycle traffic and the congestion, a cyclo driver, pedaling alongside, hassled me relentlessly to ride in his cab. Despite my repeated refusals, he nagged on.

"Where are you from?" the guy asked.

It is my least favorite question, anywhere. I didn't answer him.

"Where are you from?" he asked again.

Again I ignored him.

"You are a Nacirema," he said, and pedaled away.

"We ran over a man," someone whispered, rousing me from sleep.

"What?"

"The train just ran over a man, killing him, and we are collecting a donation for his family," the man elaborated. It was very dark inside the cubicle, and as I tried to study his square face, I noticed, for the first time, two officious-looking women standing behind him.

"Give me a moment, okay?" I told him as I fished a bundle of bills from inside my jeans pocket. Five dollars? No, two. "Here," I said as I handed over 20,000 dong (an equivalent of a good day's wage there).

"Thank you."

After they left, I thought it would really be funny if, in the morning, I asked one of the men in the next cubicle about the accident, only to be told, "What accident?"

"I think," the skinny guy from the next cubicle said, "that it was probably a suicide, since no one would be lying on the tracks at that hour of night, although people do do that during the daytime."

"Maybe he was drunk," I suggested.

"That's possible," the skinny guy conceded, puffing on his 555. "Or maybe he was already dead. That's another possibility. Maybe someone killed him and left his body on the tracks."

The old man, who was listening, chimed in: "On my way up, we also ran over a guy; however it was clearly his fault, since he ignored the barrier at the crossing and tried to speed his Honda across the tracks."

"Stupid," the skinny guy said, shaking his head. Then: "There goes a Honda Dream! Two thousand bucks down the drain!" We all laughed.

Inspired by the general gaiety, I said, "You know, a hangover can make you feel so shitty that death might be preferable."

The skinny guy stared at me. "This guy's all right. He's insane!"

"Drink up, everybody," the old man urged as he filled our cups.

"Listen," the skinny guy said, then sang:

> *"One cup, eyes open wide.*
> *Two cups, eyes start to droop.*
> *Three cups, start talking trash.*
> *Four cups, yell: I'm the king!*
> *Five cups, fondle the dog.*
> *Six cups, think prick is head.*
> *Seven cups, sleep in the street."*

And so the dead man drank seven cups, stumbled onto the tracks on his way home, passed out, and was run over. Although this theory was no more plausible than the other two, I was personally in favor of it because, while it would make his demise absolutely senseless, it would also hold him to be entirely responsible.

I made an analogous mistake only a few hours later. Taking up the old man's offer, I drank at least a dozen cups of his hideous wine and was completely fucked up by the time we pulled into Ho Chi Minh City. Eager to get off the train, and in my altered state, I completely forgot about a plastic bag containing my rolls of film. The dead man lost his one roll of film. I lost twenty. One minute I was drinking and laughing, the next minute I was standing on the street. I thus lost, in one careless moment, all the impressions I'd been greedily hoarding for the previous thirty days.

■ SAIGON PULL

Across a narrow lake from my house in the center of Hanoi is a hideous-looking hotel named Saigon Pull. Built four years ago, it features a floating disco, a tinseled, strobe-lit barge that blares loud music until three o'clock each morning. Although I tried jamming wads of rolled-up newspaper into my ears, the monotonous *thump, thump, thump* still filtered through. Once I even tried bandaging the top half of my head.

However, this floating disco is not just a nuisance but a windfall. It is where my only daughter, Lai, works as a hostess. She brings home, on average, fifteen dollars a night, half the monthly wage of your average teacher.

With this income I no longer have to leave the house. Before Lai became a hostess my family survived on what I could make from selling Zippo lighters, supplemented by my tiny pension.

I had several designs for my Zippo lighters. My favorite one read, "When I Die, Bury Me Upside Down So the World Can Kiss My Ass."

It can be translated as: "When I Die, Bury Me Upside Down So the World Can Kiss My Ass."

I would sit on the sidewalk across the street from the Metropole Hotel, in front of a hand towel arrayed with six Zippo lighters. (There were dozens more in my satchel.) It was prudent not to show too many at one time. That way they became rare. I would sell each for five, maybe six dollars. Once, a strangely emotional man, with tears in his eyes, paid me twenty dollars although I only asked for ten.

I would also carve, for a small, negotiable fee, a tropical scene, someone's name, or a simple greeting in French or English onto any solid surface with my penknife. Look at this cheap plastic pen, for example: See the fruit-laden coconut tree, the sun sinking into the ocean, and above it, "Good Night, My Love!"

Now I stay home all day to take care of my three-year-old grandson, Tuan. There are only three of us in my family: me, Lai, and Tuan.

Tuan is a big-boned and precocious child. Already he can recite the alphabet, forward and backward, and count to a hundred. I have taught him a few fancy words. Once, when my neighbor, Mr. Truong, was over for a beer, I said, "Tuan, tell Mr. Truong what's inside the body?"

Tuan looked at me blankly. I nudged. "You know, the tiny little things no one can see."

He still didn't get it. I gave him a hint: "GGGGGGGGGG! GGGGGGGGGGGGGG!"

"Germs?"

"See." I looked at Mr. Truong. "He already knows the word germs!"

Mr. Truong was laughing convulsively. His one good eye narrowed into a slit slithering up toward the top of his nose. His mouth nearly slid off his face. "This kid speaks excellent Vietnamese!"

Encouraged, I pointed to a photograph on the wall. "And who's that?"

"Uncle Ho!"

"And what about Uncle Ho?"

"Uncle Ho loves children!"

After Mr. Truong left, I thought of how glad I was that Mr. Truong seemed to genuinely like my grandson and had never made an off-color remark about Tuan in my presence.

Well, almost never. One time, after seeing Tuan kick a rubber ball across the floor, he raised his hands in the air and yelled, "Pelé!"

It is true that Mr. Truong likes to make a lot of far-fetched comparisons. He said that Hanoi is becoming more and more like New York. (He has never been anywhere near New York. Indeed, never outside of Vietnam.) He calls Lai "a famous actress," and me "the general." He said, "You look just like Vo Nguyen Giap." An absurd comparison, preposterous. As is clear in every photograph, and I've even met the great man once, with a photograph in my wallet to prove it, General Giap has a round, well-marbled, toadlike face, while yours truly's is gaunt, meatless, with eyes that bug out just a little. I have a bushy mustache, and General Giap does not. Although General Giap's nose is mashed, beaten down, smoothed over, it does retain its full complement of accessories, while yours truly's, I'm sorry to say, *excusez-moi*, is missing a nostril. Furthermore, everyone knows that Vo Nguyen Giap is only four-nine, one of the shortest men in the universe, and I was, swear to God, a very tall guy. Perhaps Mr. Truong is implying that in my current abbreviated version, I'm about the size of Vo Nguyen Giap.

I've already decided that Tuan would never be sent to school. Why subject him to other children's cruelty? I've talked to Lai about this. After she quits what she's doing—Lai's already twenty-five—she can open a beauty salon. We'll call it Paris By Night. Plucked eyebrows, perms, and nails. Tuan can help out at the shop when he's old enough, and be a beautician when he's fully grown.

Each night, just before bed, I rub egg yolk into Tuan's hair to straighten it out. I don't know if it will work, but it's worth a try. I've also been telling him to pinch his flaring nostrils, massaging them, to get them to rise up.

"Do it twenty times, Tuan."

"But why, Grandpa?"

"Because it's good for your nose!" At the end of each nose session, I give Tuan a generous handful of M&M's. Imported stuff, very expensive.

Mrs. Buoi, the pudding vendor down the street, told me that the American singer, Michel Jason, soaks his body in a bathtub of fresh milk every day to achieve a light complexion. Condensed milk doesn't work, she added.

A nha que ignoramus, Mrs. Buoi should stick to peddling pudding and stop dishing out advice on the latest advances in science and cosmetics. Besides, even a pint of milk costs well over a dollar. There's no way I'm spending all of Lai's earnings on fresh milk. I had thought of getting a pint of milk and dabbing Tuan, just the crucial spots, maybe just the tops of his hands and the front of his face, with a hand towel. But if I apply this treatment unevenly, he'll end up looking all mottled, like a tree frog or a napalm victim. It's not worth the risk is what I say.

But who am I to brand Mrs. Buoi a *nha que* ignoramus? What pomposity! I should scratch the scars on my face until they bleed to atone for such a statement! Show me a Vietnamese, even the most *au courant, c'est moi* included, who isn't a generation, at most two, removed from being a *nha que* ignoramus?

For all I know, you yourself are a *nha que* ignoramus. Perhaps, just this morning, you were standing ankle-deep in mud, planting rice seedlings with your ass aimed skyward? It's nothing to be ashamed of. So what if you have never eaten M&M's or bought a roll of toilet paper in your life?

You should be proud to be *au naturel, parlez-vous Français?* like a heron or a water buffalo. You should be proud to be the heir to a million folk poems no one can remember. You should be proud to be a repository of occult knowledge city slickers like me are clueless about. (Like Mr. Truong said, Hanoi is becoming more and more like New York, less and less like the rest of Vietnam.) If I look at you the wrong way, you can cause a bag of nails or a live duck to appear in my poor stomach. Because you stand in the sun all day, planting rice seedlings with your ass aimed skyward, you are robust, slightly crazed, and dark-complexioned. You know, from experience, that skin color is not constant but variable. What is skin pigment but germs that can be bleached with the right chemical?

When I first suggested the beauty salon idea to Lai, she seemed deeply ambivalent, even afraid. When something's troubling her, Lai's lips will jut out a little, as if she's getting ready to kiss someone she does not really want to kiss. She would also tilt her head back and blink her eyes rapidly. A *jolie laide,* my Lai is. I reassured her: "Don't worry, don't worry, I promise to never show up at your shop."

"What are you talking about?!" She protested, tilting her head back and blinking rapidly.

"Oh, come on, it's a beauty salon! Why would people want to see a monster in a beauty salon?"

It is true that the new generation has very little tolerance for ugliness, for whatever that is unglamorous, maimed, unphotogenic. All reminders of the war embarrass them. The war itself embarrasses them. It was a huge aberration, they've decided. (And they're right, of course, but then they blame people like me for having participated in it, as if we had any choice in the matter.) They see the cash-friendly Americans on the street and cannot imagine why we ever fought them.

Each night, not being able to sleep, I lie in the dark inside the mosquito netting next to my grandson and remember incidents from my generic, yet harrowing life. Only now, at the age of fifty-three, have I achieved boredom, a kind of peace, if not happiness. I think of my wife, of our four nights together. Some men are destined for many nights of love. I was destined for four. Flesh on flesh is a lifetime memory, they say. Each night was different. In many ways I was lucky that The Uyen, the wife I barely knew, was two years dead by the time I returned from the war. I was damaged goods, useless, a nuisance.

Or I would think of my brief glimpses of Hue, the only city aside from Hanoi I have ever been in; or the b.s. I fed the pretty reporter from Quan Doi Nhan Dan about commandeering an ARVN tank and plowing it into their own bunker—"You should have heard them scream, miss"; or the time we discovered an upturned American truck in a ravine, its driver already dead, and found, to our delight, canned ham and peaches in its cargo; or the time I stepped on an American soldier but did not shoot him, and how it bothered me for weeks afterward; or the cache of whiskey my battalion found in an overran ARVN base camp....

During my first month in the field, I saw what I thought were human entrails dangling from a tree branch above head level. All pink and gray and dripping blood. It frightened me so much I actually threw up. When I told the other soldiers about this, they all laughed. "It was a snake, you idiot!"

Lai would not usually be home until after eight in the morning. Foreign men and Viet Kieu like to sleep late, she told me. And most of them like to talk a little after they wake up, she added, even if they have to pay a little extra.

Naturally I never ask Lai about her work, although sometimes she tells me things. We have an agreement that she can never receive a man inside the house. (With Tuan here, it would not be moral.)

Once, however, a Viet Kieu showed up on one of Lai's nights off and insisted, begged, to be let in. Although the young man was very drunk, he was neither rude nor belligerent. After a little conference between Lai and me, we decided, what the heck, let the sorry bastard in.

"Thank you, Uncle, I really appreciate this," the Viet Kieu said to me in a thick Quang Ngai accent, bowing like a yo-yo with his meaty hands clasped together in front of his chest.

"It's not New Year's yet, stop kowtowing!"

"Thank you, Uncle!"

"Just treat us like family!"

So there we were, all four of us, sleeping on two beds in the one room of my house. The Viet Kieu, fully dressed, was clutching Lai as if she was the last inner tube left bobbing on the South China Sea. Great whites were swimming beneath the bed. He babbled on about his life as a solid-waste specialist in Miami, and left before sunrise.

After the Viet Kieu left, Tuan, the little booger, said, "Was that my father?"

Although the Saigon Pull is literally only a stone's throw from my house, it takes Lai fifteen minutes to ride around the lake on her Dream motorcycle. I always know she is coming when I hear Mr. Truong's Pekinese bitch's frantic barking. She always brings something from the market, sweet rice with Chinese sausage, baguettes with pâté, or vermicelli with grilled meatballs. Occasionally she also brings home foreign newspapers or magazines taken from the hotel.

Although I enjoy looking at all the photographs in these publications, even the most banal—the layout of a bathroom in a soap advertisement, for example, or the head of a hairy deer over a fireplace—what attract me most are the images of disaster: a race car bursting into flames, a riot, someone in handcuffs. It is reassuring to see people in other countries suffer, in their own house, so to speak, because the foreigners who are here now, in 1995, do not suffer.

On the front page of last week's *Bangkok Post* was a picture of a man in a red beret, khaki pants, and white T-shirt aiming, with one muscular arm, a Bulgarian SA-93 at the face of another man lying on the ground, naked but for a pair of green socks. I have seen war, but I have never seen such a tidy tableau of warfare. I had no idea which country this was in. But since both men were black, maybe somewhere in Africa. The naked man was clutching his crotch with one hand and trying to ward off the inevitable with his other. One of the socks was dangling from his foot. To the side, five teenagers hid behind a wall, with one cautiously peering out to witness this spectacle.

I have seen only one black man close up in my life. It was in a forest near Pleiku. We had ambushed an American patrol and were combing the area to scavenge weapons from the corpses before the helicopters came. I stepped over a fallen log onto something soft. Something moaned underfoot. It was a rather smallish black man, bleeding but conscious, his left arm missing. I can still see this man's face today: He had these odd little bumps on his lower cheeks and a ragged goatee. I stared at this man's eyes staring back at me. No one else was near. I kept on walking.

When Tuan was born, I immediately thought of this black man I didn't kill. A karmic joke: Since you liked the first one so much, here!, have another one. I laughed so hard at the hospital, they all thought I had gone mad.

But it did bother me for weeks afterward, the fact that I didn't, couldn't, shoot this soldier. What kind of a soldier am I if I cannot finish off my enemy?

But then I would return, over and over, to that face, a face showing neither fear nor defiance, with its little odd bumps on the lower cheeks and a sparse goatee. If anything, he seemed embarrassed. It was as if he had just woken up and was surprised to find me standing over him. A rather feminine response, I concluded, to be embarrassed after you have been violated. It was because he was caught in a compromising position, most definitely, but then so was I. It was as if I had walked into a latrine without knocking and found him squatting over the cement hole. "Excuse me, sir." But what was either one of us doing in a mosquito-infested indigo forest on such an unbelievably hot summer afternoon anyway? He with his left arm missing and covered with mud? And me with both of my legs about to be blown away forever?

■ BROTHER NEWS FROM HOME

I was the only one who could read during the war. Everyone else in my unit was illiterate. Most of us were fishermen and rice farmers from Thanh Hoa and Thai Binh provinces.

The other soldiers called me Brother News From Home. It was my job to read the letters sent from their wives, girlfriends, and mothers when these arrived every few months.

At first each soldier would bring me his letter in private. They were shy about it, almost ashamed. For my trouble, I would be paid with a cigarette, a spoonful of salt, or a sesame candy.

As we all got to know one another better, a ritual developed where I would read each letter out loud to everyone. It was our sole entertainment and consolation. Standing in the middle of a circle, with all eyes on me, I would give a dramatic performance of each missive, adding the necessary pathos, bathos, or humor through voice inflection and hand gestures.

Anyone who refused to have his letter read out loud would

be wrestled to the ground and tickled by the other soldiers until he agreed to hand over his generic secret.

There was one stubborn soldier who would light a match to his letters before anyone could see them. He was tall, muscular, but very shy. Whenever he had to look anyone in the eyes, he would bite his lip to keep from smiling.

Reading so many letters, I quickly realized that most of them were written by essentially one person: a sweet, caring, dull, and unimaginative woman. Occasionally there would be an odd detail in a letter to distinguish it from the rest. One hysterical girlfriend wrote, *They're bombing Hanoi constantly. I almost wish a bomb would drop on me. That way that same bomb would not drop on you* [!]

In another letter she wrote, *I'm certain I will die soon. How I wish you had made me pregnant. If the child survives us, then there is proof that we had lived. If the child dies, then at least more of us had lived.*

A Catholic mother wrote, *Remember to keep the statue of the Virgin Mary in your mouth when you go into battle. Wear it around your neck at all times, except when you evacuate your bowels, then you must take it off of course. Keep it in your mouth when you're sleeping.*

These peculiar details would illicit uproarious laughter from all those present. Crude comments were common. Each life, when examined publicly, seemed unbearably ridiculous. Of course the only ones who were never laughed at were those who never received any letters.

Although I was the designated letter reader, I myself never received any letters.

As a matter of ethics I would never change the contents of a letter as I was reading it, although occasionally, I would skip over unnecessary words and paraphrase long-winded passages to improve comprehension.

Only once did I break my own rule. In a rambling letter a wife admitted to her husband that she was pregnant with someone else's child. I changed it to her announcing that their house had burned down.

It was a spontaneous and harrowing performance. In front of a laughing assembly I had to improvise several hundred words without flinching. Luckily, my deceit was never found out, as the husband in question died in battle the very next day.

Because this man's letter was incinerated along with his knapsack, my integrity as a letter reader would survive intact until the very end of the war.

■ FOR GRISTLES

I'm not ignorant, because I drive a truck for a living. I've been here and there. Once I drove all the way to Lang Son, where I could look across the border into a foreign country: China. The cradle of civilization. The Chinese buildings were different. They tended to be taller, for once, and had bits of red paint on them. Chinese buildings are not the same as Vietnamese buildings. Those who claim otherwise are stupid.

Do you know that scientists used to think monkeys were vegetarians? This fact I gleaned from reading *Today's Knowledge*, a journal I highly recommend. *Today's Knowledge* now claims that monkeys are not vegetarians. They only become vegetarians in zoos. Meat is too expensive, and too messy. Recently scientists were able to videotape monkeys actually eating their own kind. A group of male monkeys had chased a monkey of a slightly different coloring onto a linden tree. They stood on the ground and shook the linden tree until the stranded monkey fell down. Then they all pounced on him and tore him to bits. The females of the tribe had been on the periphery of the action, but they, too, were able to share in the feast by trading in what you would call biblical knowledge for gristles.

No startling fact: monkeys killing monkeys. I, too, have killed a few monkeys myself, when I drove my truck down the Ho Chi Minh Trail during the war.

And just last week I accidentally killed a man when his motorbike swerved into my path. It was late at night, on the road between Soc Trang and Can Tho. Although I didn't have my headlights on (to save gas), he should have heard me coming. He didn't, of course, because he was wearing a helmet.

I should have stopped to see how he was doing after I ran over him, but I have a family to take care of: a wife with tuberculosis and a beautiful daughter about to get married to a Sri Lankan.

Do you know where Sri Lanka is?

Somewhere in Europe, I've been told. What does it matter? He offered me two thousand dollars for my daughter's hand. Truth is, I would have given her to him for next to nothing.

My daughter Hoa, age seventeen, is the most beautiful girl south of the ninth parallel.

"Daddy, do you have to get on an airplane to go to Sri Lanka?"

"Yes, you do."

"Will there be mosquitoes on an airplane?"

"There will be many mosquitoes on an airplane, but they will all be stuck to the floor because of the pressurized air."

Hoa looked worried. I continued: "Listen, you're getting married to a Sri Lankan. An older Sri Lankan, considerably older, true, but still a Sri Lankan. You're going to Europe, to an industrialized society where people work with shiny machines, and not off the land. There is no future in working off the land."

And there really is no future in working off the land. Our weather is screwed up. We didn't have a dry season this year. So much water, so many snails. That's all my neighbors talk about nowadays: the snail plague. Go see for yourself. On every rice stalk are clusters of tiny red eggs. Snail eggs.

HOPE AND STANDARDS

It used to be a big deal to go to Soc Trang. Now anyone can do it. There was this miserable, vindictive road made up of rocks and potholes, which got you to the ferry landing after about two and a half hours. This ferry went back and forth often enough, but stopped operating at 9 P.M., and sometimes even earlier, without warning, so you had to sleep on a hammock in a dingy café all night long if you didn't get back in time on your return trip.

Once I slept outside on the grass with my motorcycle chained to my ankle. I used a sheet of paper for my pillow. When I woke up in the morning, every inch of my skin was covered with mosquito bites. I had lain down worrying about ghosts and not mosquitoes. Maybe it was because I was drunk. (You tend to think of ghosts when you're drunk.) I lay on my paper pillow and stared up at the grinning moon and thought about shooting star ghosts, the variety with only a head, and entrails dangling down. I also thought about the boy in my village who had slept outside one night, only to wake up in the morning in the middle of a bamboo thicket. They had to chop through all that bamboo to get him out.

Now, with this new paved road, anyone can get to Soc Trang in less than an hour. There is no more glamour to Soc Trang. But I've been to Soc Trang dozens of times before, so it doesn't really matter to me. I know all the karaoke cafés on April 30th Street. There, you will often find me sitting in air conditioning, singing the latest hits with the prettiest hostesses. I've even been to Can Tho three times, and once I reached the outskirts of Saigon. Generally speaking, though, it takes so much effort to go anywhere. That's why many of us die in the same house we're born in.

But there is really little difference between Soc Trang, Can Tho, and the outskirts of Saigon. Everywhere there are too many people living in ugly houses. I've lived in Vinh Tho all my life, so I'm very tired of it, but I've been told by outsiders that it's a gorgeous village.

The only thing I like about Vinh Tho are the fields surrounding it. When I was a kid, I would wander the dirt roads alone late at night and pretend I was going to a foreign country. This was when there were no TVs, when we didn't know what foreign countries were like.

I used to look at the sky and think, *This sky covers the whole earth, every single country on earth, and not just this crappy village.* I also liked to look at the sea, and the many stars above it, before my family bought me a place on a boat to escape from Vietnam. That's how we ended up destitute. I was only ten then. Before we even got a mile offshore, they caught us.

Inside a pocket sewn shut into my shorts, I had three hundred dollars. "This should last you a year in America," my mother had assured me. But the cops weren't stupid. Back on land, they strip-searched us and took everything away. In the holding cell, I saw an old woman swallow a wad of dollars, a few crumpled bills at a time, before they could get to her. *It's better to turn money to shit,* her eyes said to me, *than to let these assholes steal them.*

What would I be now if I had made it to a foreign country? Maybe a taxi driver. I hear they make good money over there. As long as I don't have to talk too much, I'll be fine. Maybe I'd have my own business, something modest, a noodle shop catering to other Vietnamese.

Many people from our village did manage to escape, however, including some of the boys I grew up with. When they returned years later, they all looked rich and foreign.

Thuan was my next door neighbor. I used to beat him up all the time. He was dark and scrawny, a very ugly kid, but he escaped by boat when he was eleven. When he came back four years ago, he was this giant of a man. He stood with his legs wide apart and sat with his legs wide apart. He wore a white T-shirt with a laughing duck on it. He slapped me on the back and shouted, "How it's going?!" Easy enough for you to say.... What do you mean "how it's going"?! He bought everyone drinks at the café. "I can't drink Saigon beer"—he would frown—"always gives me a fuckin' headache! Only Tiger beer for me!" He stayed for two weeks and married the prettiest girl in our village.

It must be the cool weather that makes them so big. Near the equator, in the tropics, you sweat all your calcium and vitamins away. And it can't hurt that they drown themselves in milk and butter all day. In our village there is only yogurt. When I have children, I will make them eat a cup of yogurt a day. There are no advantages in being a little man.

Most of the pretty girls in our village have been claimed by the returning Viet Kieu, a development that has raised hope and standards. Even the ugliest girls are waiting to be hooked up with a Viet Kieu.

But no Viet Kieu has returned for a while. They are all married perhaps, some to American women no doubt. Perhaps the word is out that there are no more pretty women to be had in our village.

This past January a city woman reeking of imported perfume showed up at the Phoenix, our new six-room hotel, and stayed for two days. She would sit at a table at the edge of the market, sipping her iced coffee, and scrutinize all the young girls walking by. A crowd stood and stared at her from across the street. She had a certain way of stirring the ice in her glass that drew the ire of all those present. I was told that she offered certain girls five hundred dollars, others a thousand, to marry Taiwanese men. Incredibly, no one accepted.

We all know that any Taiwanese man who would come to Vietnam to buy a bride is probably old, crippled, or retarded, but it is sheer madness to pass up a thousand bucks and a chance to go to a foreign country. But I'm speaking from a male perspective, of course. No Viet Kieu or foreign women have ever come to our village to claim any one of us.

I may be stupid but I know this much: Any woman can get married if she would only lower her standards. This is not true for a man: He needs to have money, status, or looks, in that order.

Thao, one of the chosen ones, said to everybody, "Who wants to go to Taiwan when, with a little patience, you could go to America?"

Thao was nineteen, a real beauty, perhaps the last pretty girl in our village. She had an upturned nose and a face like a chinaberry. All her teeth were real. Her only drawback was that she had no breasts and had to wear a padded bra, although the city woman couldn't have known that.

I used to have a crush on Thao. We all did. But that was when I was just a kid, before I wised up to the ways of the world. An average guy like me can only hope to buy an illusion of love from such a pretty woman. That's why I go to Soc Trang.

I know for certain Thao wears a padded bra. We have a tradition in Vinh Tho. During the Mid-Autumn Festival, all the youths in our village form a line to do the snake dance. Alternating boy, girl, boy, girl, and holding hands, we dance in a line under the full moon around a bonfire. Married people, old people, and kids, who are not allowed to participate, cheer us on by clapping and hollering. At the climax of the dance everyone makes a big whooshing sound and the entire line collapses forward. That's your opportunity to grab the crotch of the girl behind you, and press your own crotch against the girl ahead of you. Thao was behind me and that's how I found out she wore a padded bra.

The same city woman returned to the Phoenix in May. This time she only stayed for one day. A month after she left, Thao disappeared.

We all had a good laugh over it. Taiwan turned out to be not so bad after all, but Thao, after being so stuck up, was too embarrassed to say a proper good-bye to her home village. By contrast, all the girls who married Viet Kieu had big wedding banquets where they could gloat and show off their jewelry.

Cementing our suspicion, her father immediately tore down their little thatch hut to build a little brick house. This brick house already has a nickname. People are calling it "Made In Taiwan."

Some people said her father had beaten her into making this

decision. They claimed to have heard her cry and scream in the middle of the night, but rumors are always swirling around our stupid little village, and I don't believe half of them.

The old man, being as proud as his daughter, will not reveal where his daughter has gone. He doesn't have to deal with us anymore, since he no longer has to pump tires and fix bicycles at the market. Living off the money she's sending back, no doubt, he can stay in the privacy of Made In Taiwan all day long, to get drunk and sleep and get drunk.

The wine seller, Mr. Trung, the only man who sees Thao's father regularly anymore, is letting us in on a secret. The old man has apparently told him, "No! No! No! No! My daughter did not marry a Taiwanese! We have much higher standards than that! She didn't even marry a Viet Kieu but an American. A real American! She will sacrifice her youth to suck this guy dry! Within five years we'll get a divorce. Then she'll get her American citizenship. Then she'll bring me to America. I'm not that stupid!"

■ CALIFORNIA FINE VIEW

Strange what a pair of Levy's jeans can do to a man's confidence, he thinks as he sits at a window table in the California Fine View restaurant three floors above street level. A new pair of American jeans—he smiles—expertly haggled down from thirty to just twelve bucks at Ben Thanh Market yesterday. *When I first came to the city, I couldn't even haggle,* he remembers. *I was intimidated. I used to think that if you haggle too much, they'd think you're a destitute, stupid hick. But I've certainly come a long way.* He chuckles inside. *I'm wearing Ralph Lauren's Polo Sport and a pair of leather shoes, also bought yesterday, imported from China and costing nearly a month's salary.* Suddenly his face twitches, shot through with a surge of anger. On the pastel-yellow walls are framed photos of the the Golden Gate Bridge and the Grand Canyon. *To hell with it,* he thinks, shooing the turbulence away with a quick gulp of way-too-sweet lemonade. *Not nearly enough lemon,* he concludes bitterly. *But extravagance is an occasional necessity,* he reminds himself. *You must be extravagant every now and then if you want to shift your paradigm. A very important word: paradigm. How serendipitous it was that I came across it in my very first novel.* And to think—he blushes—only a year ago I didn't even know what a novel was. Now I read at least a page every night. He smiles. *People are stuck in ruts because they have never heard of the word paradigm. And then their lives are ruined. To live beyond your means every once in a while is an act of defiance. When you're in debt, you cannot be complacent. You either sink into despair or you become creative. You must change your life,* he has read somewhere. *Renewals cost money, certainly. What bullshit,* he thinks. *I'm only dressed up to impress a woman.*

As a woman enters the room, he rises halfway out of his chair, then quickly sits down again. *And she doesn't even look like my date,* he nearly laughs inside. A glance at his watch shows that Lan is seventeen minutes late already. *Strange how different the world can look from a third-floor window. Nothing matters from up here. People are shrunken down to size, and all of life's horrors simply evaporate. But maybe it's only the air-conditioning.* Across the street a legless woman surfs along on a dolly lying on her stomach. A loudspeaker next to her head crackles a Buddhist mantra. *How odd it is that I cannot even visualize my date's face at the moment. But I do remember her name, certainly, Tran Thuy Lan, or Tran Ngoc Lan, or something like that. But if someone were to ask me anything about her appearance, for example does she wear her hair long or short, or does she wear makeup, I wouldn't be able to tell him.*

He finishes his lemonade. *Way too much ice,* he concludes bitterly. Two tables away, a young white couple are eating something extravagant: a pastry with stuff all over it. The aroma wafts over to his table. The pepperoni is real, but the cheese is fake.

He has never eaten cheese before. He waves at a waiter. "What is that?" he whispers.

"Pizza," the waiter answers. "Italian. Would you like to try it?"

He smiles in gratification. "Maybe later. But give me a Tiger beer for now."

"We only have Heineken and Budweiser."

"Say that again."

"Hei-ne-ken and Bud-wei-ser."

"Give me the first kind."

He takes out a pen and writes *pi za* in his notebook. On the same page with *parrot, pistol,* and *pajamas.* It is 7:23 P.M. He looks at the white couple again and comes to the extraordinary realization that he has never been indoors with someone of another race before. *A new paradigm.* He exhales. *I've seen them on the streets, sure, many times, but never in a room like this. The man is slovenly, even dorky-looking, but the woman is indeed gorgeous, with an extraordinarily thin nose and very red lips. The man is wearing Levi's jeans and I'm wearing Levy's jeans. I've never touched the skin of another race before.* He catches himself raking his eyeballs across the woman's baby blue T-shirt. *But why am I looking at her while waiting for my date?*

"Where are you from?" he thinks in English. *"I'm from Manchester. It is raining hard. You can either come or stay with me. I'm the most tallest person in my family. The bathroom is outside. I am healthy, you are sick." In about a year's time, I should be able to master English.* He chuckles.

He looks at his reflection in the plate glass window. "*Pi za,*" he mumbles. *Intense eyes and serious lips. Ever since I've trained myself to keep my mouth shut when not speaking, my face has become more dignified and more substantial. A minimum of thirty push-ups a night.*

Fifty when I'm not too tired. The Saigon traffic is not too bad on this overcast Sunday. A different waiter returns with his Heineken. After filling his glass, the man grins and says, "Ralph Lauren's Polo Sport!"

He reacts with an audible sniff. "Calvin Klein aftershave!"

The waiter walks away, winking over his shoulder. *A fine place this is,* he thinks. *Except for the geckos on the pastel-yellow wall of course. The whole country is overran by geckos, sure, but there should be at least one room in Vietnam where there aren't any of these flesh-colored lizards. The government should figure out a way to eradicate them. Pay kids to shoot them with rubber bands or something.* He takes a cautious sip of his imported beer.

He met Lan a week ago in the CD section of a bookstore, that enormous one on Nguyen Thi Minh Khai Street. He had come to buy his third novel—Sheldon's *Bloodline* in a fine translation. He noticed a pretty girl holding a Trinh Nam Son CD. "Buy it," he advised, "it's excellent!"

She turned to him with a twinkle in her eyes.

"I have that very CD at home," he stammered.

"I was just looking at the cover," she said cheerfully. "I don't even have a CD player!"

But it was probably a mistake to ask her to meet me at California Fine View, he now thinks. *A girl who doesn't have a CD player would probably be intimidated by a fine place like this, a well-lit place where people from all over the world gather to eat pizza and drink Heineken. Where the chairs are wood and not plastic.* But she was also wearing a jazzy and expensive blouse, he remembers, an indication that she also aspires to move up in this world.

The girl is not even here and already I'm spending beaucoup *bucks,* he laments. He looks out the window and notices that the street has turned dark suddenly. The only lights are the lights on the motorcycles. *But they have a generator here and this is a good beer.* He takes another sip.

It is 7:40 P.M. The room is crowded with black marketeers and bribe takers, noveau riche and Party officials. At a corner table a dark-skinned Indian man is eating a Greek salad. *In a single day I've rubbed elbows with both black and white people.* He congratulates himself by ordering another Heineken.

Seven fifty-six P.M. and a shoeshine boy is approaching his table. *How odd,* he thinks, *that they would allow a shoeshine boy to walk into a place like this. A barefoot third-grader sporting a harelip. At least no one is trying to sell me lottery tickets.*

"Shoeshine?"

"Sure."

The kid crawls under the table. *What the hell,* he thinks. He waves at a waiter and points at his empty bottle.

Eight twenty-five P.M., and she is definitely not coming. On the street the lights have come back on. *I'm drunk and I'm not disappointed. At least I've had a chance to experience the California Fine View. Everything in life is serendipity. If I had stayed at home, I would have learned nothing. The window of my rented room looks straight into another window across a six-foot-wide alley.* The California Fine View is now noisy with celebrating Taiwanese. Middle-aged men with teenage Vietnamese escorts. He waves at a waiter for his check.

The check tells him that by drinking three Heinekens and a lemonade alone, he has spent a week's salary. *The hell with it,* he thinks. *Extravagance is a necessity every once in a while. You must will yourself to shift your paradigm every once in a while.* He rises halfway out of his chair, then quickly sits down again. He wiggles his socked toes for a moment, then ducks his head under the table. There is nothing on the floor but a toothpick and a soiled napkin. He looks and looks but cannot find what he is looking for. When he is upright again, he sees the smiling waiter, Mr. Calvin Klein after-shave, clearing his table. "Is anything wrong?"

■ 10x50

Hua Trung. Male, 22, 5-5, 115 lbs. Dark. Bad teeth. Does odd jobs for money. Crawled into the sewer a few days ago. If made 20,000 in the morning, will spend 4,000 on noodles in the afternoon then gamble away the rest. When eighteen, molested a five-year-old girl.

Ly Lan. Female, 23, 5-6, 124 lbs. Wears padded bras. Always joking about money. Often donates money to Buddhist temples. Gets boys to spend money on her, then leaves them. Will probably marry a Taiwanese twice her age with a missing limb. Speaks Vietnamese, Chinese, and ten words of English.

Tran Nam Thai. Male, 31, 5-3, 98 lbs. Rejected by the army for not meeting weight requirement. Buys rusty jeep parts, then resells them. Has a son in America he's never seen. Does not talk, but honks (with lips sticking out). Wears CK aftershave. Dates a girl who sells pork.

Nguyen Thi Thom. Female, 21, 5-4, 130 lbs. Incompetent, illiterate domestic servant. Sleeps on the floor next to a black dog. Slurs every other word. Giggles whenever anyone says "love." Has memorized the name of every Hong Kong movie actor. Father is a violent drunk. Very interested in Hua Trung.

Duong Quang Long. Male, 26, 5-8, 145 lbs. Cocaine addict. Likes to surf the Internet and go to "a beer and a hug" cafés. Has a tomboyish daughter. Pregnant wife swallowed pills a month ago in an attemped suicide. Does not come home most nights. Very fond of gold fish.

Doan Thi Hoai. Female, 19, 5-2, 106 lbs. Placed next-to-last in the neighborhood fashion show. Likes to wear see-through blouses in the evening. Has never seen the ocean, a mountain, a horse, or someone of another race. Works in a shoe factory. Is saving to buy a bicycle.

Nguyen Manh Tuan. Male, 38, 5-4, 127 lbs. A strict vegetarian. Has a room in his house devoted to the Goddess of Mercy. Said to have a tiny penis. In early youth, hit on every boy in the neighborhood. A fan of Michael Jackson and Renaldo. Has sworn off pornography.

Bui Phung Hoa. Female, 43, 4-10, 96 lbs. A lifelong Communist and a virgin. Good with numbers. Although first love escaped by boat from Vietnam twenty years ago, still stares at his photographs regularly. Likes to copy a long poem into a notebook before sleep. Enjoys scrutinizing maps and dictionaries.

Nguyen Huy Loc. Male, 40, 5-7, 141 lbs. Sleeps with older women for money. Estranged from wife. Always fantasizing about emigrating to Australia to become a sheep farmer. Once locked self inside a darkened room for two months to draw pornographic pictures on the walls with a crayon. A poet.

Vu Thanh Thao. Female, 32, 5-1, 108 lbs. Has three children fathered by two men, four abortions. Finished last in the neighborhood fashion show. In early youth, was convinced she would become a famous singer. Was mistress to a famous Buddhist monk for a year. Paints nails for a living.

■ THE HIPPIE CHICK

As my father would have said, "It don't make no logical sense, spending half an hour to save a nickel." We were sitting on beach chairs on a cement-floored veranda facing the South China Sea. Across the Pacific Ocean was our ranch home in Oregon, a mere dot on the hazy horizon. Directly in front of us, across a wobbly card table, was a platoon of peddlers. Mostly women and children, they were hawking everything from postcards of Halong Bay—a thousand miles to the north—to mangosteens, to guavas, to pirated copies of Marguerite Duras's *The Lover,* to tiny tortoises made from snail shells Super Glued together. As my wife haggled, her face appeared distressingly old, her voice mournful and threatening at the same time. Although I couldn't understand a word of what she was saying, the language, as usual, was getting on my nerves. Back home we only spoke English to each other. (Or, rather, back home we only spoke a permutation of English to each other.) The haggling had picked up in intensity. Vietnamese seems to have been invented specifically for haggling. That, and Spanish. Before we came to Vietnam, I'd never seen my wife haggle.

Shut up already, I thought, but said nothing. I smiled. My wife shot me a quick glare. I picked up my mug of Tiger beer and chug-a-lugged its content, ice cubes included, in one determined draft, spilling a third of it on my sunburned chest. Flakes of curled skin were entangled in my chest hair. It felt good to have cold beer on my toasted chest. I smiled again. My wife returned to her haggling, allowing me to steer my gaze toward the hippie chick, who was lying on the beach about fifty feet away.

The hippie chick had propped herself up onto her elbows. I had seen her for the first time only the night before, at the Inside Outside Bar, chatting up the young bartender in a mishmash of Vietnamese and English while drinking Bailey's Irish Cream. She had a droning, lisping voice caused by two decades of bong hits. Wearing a low scoop-necked blouse, she would lean over the bar periodically, and dramatically, to remind us all that she was bra-less. She was not sitting on her stool but *squatting* on it—I'm not sure why. Judging from the crow's-feet, she was at least thirty-five, and from her accent, Australian. And a world-class swimmer too, I must add.

There were no babes on the beach except for the hippie chick. A dozen schoolgirls were splashing in shorts and T-shirts. An old lady marched into the surf in her floral pajamas. Venice Beach it wasn't.

Sensing my stare, the hippie chick tilted her head back and smiled. A grotesque upside-down smile. *To hell with it,* I thought, *what had happened had already happened. I did not actually do anything wrong…. She was at least partially responsible. I was bombed. We were the only two white people on Strawberry Beach.*

I had been extremely good, angelic even, for nearly a month, ever since we arrived in Vietnam, so it was very unfortunate that, with only a few more days to go, what happened had to happen.

I had certainly had my opportunities.

During our first night in Saigon, as I was circling the block of our hotel, disoriented, two prostitutes, working in tandem, jumped my bones. I was pretending to examine the façade of a huge colonial building, a theater of some sort, when a tiny hand with a very firm grip yanked me off the sidewalk and onto a moped. Before I knew what had happened, I was sandwiched in between two perfumed women and taken on a mile-long joyride.

They dragged me into a little house cocooned in an alley. There was almost nothing in the room. On the lime-green wall was a year-old calendar—1997—and the rayon sheet on the square bed had a printed pattern of cartoon whales, penguins, and giraffes. No air-conditioning. The hum of air-conditionings was the most reassuring sound in Vietnam. It meant that you were away from the rabble. I gave them a twenty-dollar bill just to leave me alone. "No! No!" I shouted, raising my hands, palms outward, to shoulder level. "No! No!"

They were certainly doable, very beautiful and very young also, but I did absolutely nothing, even after they had taken all their clothes off.

Those two girls were yakking and giggling to each other, and in the nude, too, so of course I was provoked, but I do love my wife dearly, and that's the honest truth.

Mai Lan, that's my wife's name (some people call her Amy), was a student in my ESL class. That's how I met her. It was my first (and last) stab at charity work, and I was certainly not a very good teacher. The agency promptly let me go after a semester. It wasn't entirely my fault. The students were idiots. Most of them were obstinately slow in picking up on even the most basic instructions: the past is past tense, adjectives before nouns. Laotians, Pakistanis, Ethiopians, etc., some were probably illiterate even in their own language.

Not to imply that Mai Lan was an illiterate, but she would be confused by very basic words, such as *me* and *you,* and use them interchangeably. Likewise *yesterday* and *tomorrow.* At first I thought it was some sort of philosophical flimflam, a poker-face witticism, before I realized that she was not capable of witticism. One day Mai Lan approached me after class and said, apropos of nothing, "Morning coffee in my home?"

We were married less than a month later. No ambivalence. No tunnel warfare between the sexes. No nothing. She wanted a green card and a husband. I wanted a wife. Just like that, we became man and wife.

Mai Lan was twenty-eight at the time. I was forty. Man to man, I will confide to you that she was a virgin. No joke. There was blood on my dick.

Not that it mattered, but considering the fact that in our society, by the time you're thirty, you have slept with at least a hundred individuals already, creatures of every ilk imaginable: straight, gay, bi, bipolar, infants, seniors, dogs, and so forth, it was refreshing to meet someone who was genuinely *clean.*

But maybe Mai Lan was, and is, an illiterate. (She was certainly one of the worst students in my class.) I have never seen her read a book or a newspaper. And even now, three years into our marriage, we can hardly converse for more than a few seconds at a time. What does it matter, anyway, since there are so many other ways to channel one's affection?

My wife's broken English, to me, is her most endearing trait.

One of the biggest shocks I had coming to Vietnam was in discovering how talkative Mai Lan actually is. In her own language she could babble on to almost anyone. It was disturbing to detect a whole new range of expressions on her face. The nuances and complexities. I found myself keeping an uneasy tab on this development, to store away her hidden repertoire for my future reference in the United States.

Enough of this haggling, I thought. I stood up. "I'm going into the water."

"Go ahead!"

I tiptoed quickly over the hot sand. The hippie chick was lying perfectly still, apparently sleeping. She had to be exhausted from all that swimming the night before. "You'll never catch me," she had shouted, her head a bobbing blur in the moonlit water. I had known that she was naked although I could not prove it.

She had toyed with me. The hippie chick would disappear for a very long time, then buoy up, suddenly, on my right, then left, then right, then left, laughing the whole time. She knew I had no chance. Most of the time I was just floating in place, trying to figure out where the hell she was at. She even had the balls to grab me from below, trying to yank my shorts down! I kicked my leg out instinctively but struck nothing. How that girl managed to see underwater I'll never know. When I could no longer see the blinking lights from the beach, I freaked out and had to swim back.

It was a miracle I didn't drown. Or maybe I did drown: When I came to, I was sprawled on the sand, facedown, *with my shorts lying near my right ear.* The sun was rising. Good thing I wasn't arrested.

What had set me off was the bartender saying, "That girl swims every night. She don't mind and we don't mind."

"What do you mean by that?"

"Skinny-dip." He laughed.

"Skinny-dipping?!"

"Sure!"

"No clothes?"

The bartender gave me a look of contempt, as if I was too stupid to understand my own language. "Yes, yes, no clothes!"

I remember becoming infuriated. For a moment I thought I was going to slam my Tiger beer against the side of his face. As if on cue, all the other men sitting at the bar, all Vietnamese, started laughing. Why were they laughing?

But of course I knew why they were laughing. As I walked across the burning sand, I glanced down at her freckled cleavage and thought, *Past is past tense, adjectives before nouns.* She opened her green eyes and grinned. *Maybe I should step on your belly,* I thought. *So you won! So what?* As my wife's shrill voice pricked my sunburned back, I strode defiantly into the warm water and started swimming east.

◼ WESTERN MUSIC

Outside the glass door of Fish and Chick, the white noise of the motorcycle traffic sputtered: *putt, putt, putt, putt*. Inside, Skinny and Dercum sat at the bar, their sweat cooled by the air-conditioning. Kurt Cobain was screaming on the stereo. It was the beginning of summer, just before the monsoon season. Skinny was drunk on Jägermeister. He shouted, "I'm sick of this place!"

"So am I!" Dercum said.

"I've got to get out of here."

"We can go have a beer at M.I.G. or Bar Nixon if you like."

"No! No! No! No! What I mean is, I'm sick of Hanoi!"

"Do you want to go back to New York?"

"I don't want to go home. I just need to get away from Hanoi."

"We can go to Sapa."

"No, not Sapa." Skinny took a drag on his Perfume River cigarette. He jabbed his face over his shoulder toward the Israelis,

Dutch, Germans, Aussies, and Frenchmen sitting at tables behind them. "I'm tired of looking at these Eurotrash!"

"I'll talk to Mai tomorrow."

For five dollars a day, Mr. Mai waited every day for Dercum outside the Victory Hotel to take him where he wanted to go. He was Dercum's personal cyclo driver. Wiry, with a bronze complexion, he was in his midfifties, a grandfather. He was too well dressed for his profession. In public he wore a tailored shirt, tie, polyester slacks, and imitation leather wingtips. Unlike most men his age, he was not a veteran. He was not allowed to serve, because his parents were branded reactionaries by the Viet Minh, who executed his father in 1955 during the Land Reform Program. His mother committed suicide soon afterward.

Dercum walked out of the hotel lobby and found him, as usual, lounging in his cab beneath the flame tree. "*Chao Ong!*"

Mr. Mai roused himself from his seat: "How are you doing this morning, Dirt? Where we going?"

"I don't know yet. Maybe nowhere."

"Nowhere very good. I sit here and drink beer." Mr. Mai eased back down, lifted a plastic cup of beer to his lips. His eyes were bloodshot.

Dercum lit a Marlboro. "My friend is getting sick of Hanoi."

"Skin Knee sick of Hanoi?"

"Yes, Skinny is very sick of this place."

"Tell him to go home."

"But he does not want to go home yet."

"Tell him to go to Hanoi Hilton."

"Now, now, let's not get personal. Skinny is sick of looking at the Eu-ro-trash."

"Year-old trash?"

"Eu-ro-trash. Like White Trash." Dercum smiled good-naturedly. "Like me, but Eu-ro-pean."

Mr. Mai finished his beer, burped, crossed his leg.

Dercum continued: "We want to go the countryside, somewhere where there's no Europeans or Americans."

Mr. Mai jiggled his empty cup. "For how long, Boss?"

"A week."

"To do what?"

"Do nothing. We just want to relax in the countryside."

Mr. Mai jiggled his cup, thought for a moment, then said, "We can go to my wife's home village."

"Where's that?"

"Three hundred kilometers from Hanoi."

"Nine hours by car?"

"Ten."

"Which direction?"

"West."

"In the mountains?"

"Yes."

"Near Son La?"

"Between Son La and Yen Chau."

"Is there a hotel there?"

"Hotel?!"

Dercum called Skinny at the Metropole. "It's all arranged. We're going to the sticks for a week."

"Sounds excellent."

"You should bring along cans of Spam as a precaution."

"Don't worry. I've eaten ox penises and dogs."

"You have?"

"And sparrows."

"What else have you eaten?"

"Wouldn't you like to know."

"And we should bring along seven cases of beer. A case for each day."

"I'm really looking forward to this."

"I'll bring the toilet paper."

Dercum Sanders and Skinny, whose real name was Dave Levy, had met at Columbia. Dercum never finished college but dropped out after his sophomore year. First he worked as a bike messenger, then as a sous-chef at Coûte Que Coûte in Midtown, then as a luggage handler for United Airlines, which allowed him to travel to Asia for free, and then his grandmother died. Before Dercum left New York, he said he was going to Vietnam to teach English, but after his first week in Hanoi, he thought, *Why should I feel apologetic about not working? Why shouldn't I just hang out?* After six months in Vietnam he sent a fax to Skinny: *"You must come over soon. This place is wild. COMPLETE FREEDOM. One feels uninhibited here. I feel like a new man. I am a new man. I cannot wait to see your face again. I think about you day and night. I mean it. In New York nothing is possible. Now I see my past in a new light. You must come over."*

It took Mr. Mai three days to make arrangements for the trip. Dercum and Skinny would split the cost of hiring a four-wheel drive, at six hundred dollars a week, gas and driver included. The party would be composed of Dercum, Skinny, the driver, and Mr. Mai.

To avoid traffic, they decided to leave first thing in the morning. The car showed up promptly at 5 A.M. in front of the Victory Hotel. It was a Jeep Cherokee. They started loading. Dercum said to Mr. Mai, "All this beer is for you."

Mr. Mai stared at the cases of Heineken filling the luggage compartment and shook his head convulsively, "Not enough!"

"Not enough?!" Dercum shouted with feigned astonishment. Everyone laughed except the driver, a burly, bearded man in jeans and a pale blue T-shirt with "Mountain Everest Is The Highest Mountain In The World" on the front and "Solo Fucker" on the back.

"You want a beer now?" Dercum asked Mr. Mai.

"Sure." Dercum handed him a beer. "And one for the driver."

Dercum handed a beer to the driver.

"Thank you, mate!" the driver said.

"Mr. Mai, please tell him that we're not Australians."

"They're not Australians."

"I'm Dercum." Dercum shook the driver's hand.

Mr. Mai interjected, "Dirt!"

"It's actually 'Dirk.'"

"Dirt," the driver said.

"And this is Skinny."

"Skin Knee."

"What is your name?"

"Long." On closer inspection, Long appeared to be only about thirty, although his beard and scowl had made him seem much older.

"Long?"

"Long."

Skinny looked at Dercum with a twinkle in his eyes. "How long?" he blurted. Dercum burst out laughing. Long stared at Mr. Mai, his face blank.

"Never mind," Dercum said.

"I think I want a beer also," Skinny said.

"I didn't know you drink beer at five in the morning," Dercum said as he handed Skinny a Heineken.

"Skin Knee is becoming Vietnamese," Mr. Mai exclaimed.

Dercum and Skinny sat in the back. Mr. Mai sat up front. All except Long were elated as the car started moving. At that hour the streets were filled with people of all ages: walking, jogging, doing tai chi, kicking a soccer ball or a shuttlecock, or playing badminton. They passed a squadron of legless men rolling briskly down Le Hong Phong Street on wheelchairs. "Old V.C.," Mr. Mai said. Long tapped a morselike staccato on his horn. On the tape deck was Louis Armstrong singing Fats Waller: "*What did I do… to be so black and blue?*"

"Do you like Louis Armstrong, Mr. Mai?" Dercum asked.

Mr. Mai didn't answer him. He was suddenly withdrawn, reflective, charmed by the sights of his home city. Each scene was made novel from the vantage point of a speeding car.

"I like jazz and blues," Long said.

Most of the motor traffic they encountered was going the other way: people coming into the city from outlying villages. Within twenty minutes, the houses thinned out on both sides. Long tapped on his horn constantly, passing motorcycles, bicycles, trucks, buses, and cars while dodging chickens, pigs, cows, dogs, men, and buffalo. After three hours the road turned to gravel. Mr. Mai rolled the window down four times to throw up his three cans of beer.

Long said, "Easy, Grandfather."

Mr. Mai moaned, "I'm not used to sitting in a car."

Dercum said, "We should stop for lunch soon, Long."

Long turned his head around. "Good place to eat: twenty minutes." The car ran over a dog. Long could see a rapidly diminishing black shape twitching in the rearview mirror.

"Sounds good."

"Twenty minutes."

"Boys! I think we just ran over a dog!" Skinny yelped.

"Did we just run over a dog, Long?" Dercum asked.

"No."

"Can I have another beer?" Mr. Mai said.

Long drove the Cherokee onto the side of the road. The little eatery was fronted by a pool table beneath a fiberglass awning propped up by bamboo poles. They walked past a glass cabinet displaying imported liquors and cigarettes, stepped over a dozing yellow dog, and entered a bright, airy room. On its lime-colored walls were posters of busty white women hugging enormous beer bottles. Up high in one corner was a shelf-altar: In front of a framed, retouched black-and-white photograph of a handsome, smooth-faced, doe-eyed cadet was a sand-filled teacup holding joss sticks, a plate of mandarin oranges, and a plate of boiled chicken. At the back of the room a very old woman sat, all bunched up and immobile, on a bamboo settee in front of a very large, very loud TV, watching a soap opera. They sat down on little plastic stools at a low table. They were the only patrons. The waitress came out of the kitchen and said, "Today we have fried catfish and wild boar."

Mai ordered: "Bring those dishes, Sister. And fried tofu; boiled watercress; two bowls of soup."

"What nationality are these people, Uncle?"

"American."

"They look like Russians."

"They're gay."

"Gay!"

"Hurry up, Sister, we are all starving to death!"

The waitress went back to the kitchen.

"What did you tell her?" Skinny asked Mai.

"She said you look Russian. I said you are Americans."

Dercum asked, "Where are we?"

"Thao Nguyen."

Long said to Mai, "Are they really gay?"

"Of course!"

A gaggle of giggling children stood outside the restaurant to stare at Skinny and Dercum. Skinny smiled at them and said, "Boo!" The bravest of the children separated himself from the group and, with goading from the rest, shouted in English, "I love you!" before running away. The rest of them scattered, screaming, "I love you! I love you!"

Everyone but Skinny sat at the table picking their teeth with toothpicks after the meal. The waitress wiped the table cursorily with a rag, sweeping the little fish bones onto the tiled floor. She was wearing a lurid pink shirt with little black dots and red flowers. On her hair was a bright yellow bow. Long said to her, "Sister, do you want to go to the mountain with us?"

"There is nothing but ghosts and savages in those mountains!" She smiled and walked back to the kitchen.

In college Skinny and Dercum were not lovers. Each refused to acknowledge the unbearable fact of his attraction to the other by frantically trying to become a heterosexual. They dated many women, overlapping on occasions. (Skinny would sometimes think, as he was making love to a woman, *His penis has been in there too.*) But they remained emotional intimates, returning to each other for comfort after each failed relationship. When Dercum left for Vietnam, Skinny had just come out. Dercum was still undecided. Their love was consummated in Skinny's suite at the Metropole Hotel a day after his arrival.

The car climbed steadily. The road was mostly bad, alternating between asphalt, dirt, and gravel. They passed tea plantations, a litchi forest, fields of maize and fields of tobacco. They drove through Viet towns of wooden and whitewashed brick houses; Black Thai *bans* of houses on stilts, with cows and buffalo beneath them; a Kha Mu village of thatch-roofed huts with walls of woven bark. In every Viet town there was at least one café with a sign outside advertising "karaoke." They saw a group of Flower Hmongs. One of the men carried a flintlock rifle. The women had woven horsehair into their own hair, creating enormous turbans. Neither Skinny nor Dercum said anything for a long time. Long glanced at the rearview mirror: The two men were asleep leaning against each other.

Mr. Mai said, "How long have you been a driver?"

"Just a year."

"It seems like a great job."

"You get to see places."

"And you get to meet foreigners."

Long chuckled. "There are classy foreigners, but there are some who are impossible to deal with."

"Like who?"

"Last week I drove three Koreans. They were very unfriendly."

"How are the Americans?"

"They're actually not bad. Most of them tip."

"Any women?"

"Huh?"

"You know, you meet any women?"

Long chuckled. "A couple."

Mr. Mai waited for Long to continue. Long continued: "Most of them travel with a husband or a boyfriend. And then you have the old and Christian ones, who travel in pairs, but every now and then you catch yourself an odd single."

Mr. Mai waited for Long to continued. Long continued: "For example, a couple months ago I drove three people from New Zealand: a couple and a single girl, all college students. I drove them to Sapa, where we stayed in two rooms at the Auberge. The girl's name was Hillary. She was my girlfriend for a week."

Mr. Mai, with a pained look on his face, made an unconscious sucking sound with his throat.

Long chuckled. "I evened the score a little, you know."

"Ah." Mr. Mai sighed. "But I'm an old man, and a grandfather."

"And then there was this other one. American. Becky her name was. After I drove her to Halong Bay on a day trip, I would come to her hotel in Hanoi three or four times a week for a month. She was a sex maniac, this Becky was. 'I'm not your girl-friend,' she said, 'I just want sex.' 'Fine with me,' I said. She was sleeping with at least two or three other guys, as far as I could tell. This girl couldn't get enough of it. She was delirious. She asked me, 'Am I pretty?' 'Sure you are,' I told her. And she was pretty. Maybe not that pretty, but pretty. She told me one night, 'I'm a very ugly girl, a very ugly girl.' She was actually crying over this, that's how crazy she was."

"Maybe in America they don't think she's so pretty."

Long furrowed his brows. He wasn't sure whether to become angry.

"You know, it's the same with some of the Vietnamese girls we see hanging on the arms of foreigners. We think these girls are ugly, but the foreigners think they're very pretty. They think some of these girls the most beautiful on the face of this earth." Mr. Mai glanced at the back seat: "At least these two," he lowered his voice, "are not *corrupt*ing the chaste women of Vietnam with their decadent imperialistic materialistic pollution!"

"Ha! ha!"

"Actually these two guys don't seem to like other white people. They requested that I take them somewhere where there's no Americans."

Long was glad the conversation had veered away from his sex life. *What a dirty old man this Mai is,* he thought. "But the whole country is crawling with Americans."

"That's true."

"If not live ones, then dead ones."

"That's true."

"How do you know there's no Americans in Muom Village?"

"I've been there three times. It's my wife's native village."

"How did she end up in Hanoi?"

"I kidnapped her!"

"Ha! ha!"

"Actually my wife served in the army. That's how she made it to Hanoi."

"I figured."

"In my family the decorated veteran is a woman!"

"Ha! ha!"

"Hey, it worked out great for me: If she'd been near her family, there would've been no way they would have let her marry me."

"And how do they treat you now?"

"Like shit!"

"Ha! ha!"

"Stop for a second."

Long stopped the car to let Mr. Mai out. Dercum opened his eyes, saw the back of Long's head, forgot where he was, panicked, recovered, closed his eyes again. Long thought, *What a concept: gay Americans!!! But they all seem so... so... so... thick! So macho! All body hair and meat and sweat and swagger. Well, maybe not the Skin Knee guy.... Were gays allowed in the U.S. Army? Can there be such a thing as a gay imperialist?* Mr. Mai climbed back in. "I feel much better."

After they started moving again, Mr. Mai said, "You know, Brother, there's an American ghost in Muom Village."

"Really?"

"My wife said that, in '69, a plane was shot down over Muom Village and they found the pilot's leg in the forest."

"Just his leg?"

"Yes, but it was a very big leg. My wife told me it was as tall as a man's chest. This guy was a giant."

"They're all giants."

"But this guy was really a giant."

"People tend to be shorter in the mountains anyway."

"It's the lack of nutrients."

"No sodium."

"That's right. The villagers buried this leg where they found it, but his ghost began to show up at night, knocking on people's doors and asking for water."

Long took a sip from his Heineken. "Why do ghosts ask for water anyway?"

"Not all ghosts. Only the ones who have lost a lot of blood while dying."

"And did his entire body show up, or just his leg?"

"What do you mean?"

"When he knocked on people's doors at night, what did people see: a leg, or the entire body?"

"You really don't know?"

"No, I don't."

Mr. Mai raised his voice. "When you die, it doesn't matter if all that's left of you is your asshole, you come back as a whole person."

"I didn't know that."

"That's because you grew up in the city."

"You're right. There are no ghosts in the city."

"There are a few, but not many. There are not many ghosts in the city because of electricity."

"Tell me more about the American ghost."

"This guy kept bothering the villagers, always showing up at night and asking for water, so they went back to the burial site and erected a little shrine. After that he stopped bothering them."

"He's getting more than he deserves for dropping bombs on them." Long chuckled.

"But you can't hold a grudge against a dead man. I've seen this shrine: There was a bottle of wine and a cassette player."

"A cassette player?"

"Yes, a cassette player playing Soviet music."

"Why Soviet music?"

"Because they didn't have tapes of American music. This was in 1989, in a place where 'monkeys cough, herons crow,' where 'dogs eat rocks, chickens eat pebbles!'"

"Whose idea was it to play him music?"

"I don't know. But it makes sense if you think about it. They probably thought that since he was so far away from home, he would appreciate hearing some Western music."

Dercum made a little noise. Without opening his eyes he said, "Are we almost there, Mr. Mai?"

"We're almost there."

"The only Americans I want to see this week are these two guys back there," Long said. "I don't want to see any ghost."

"Don't worry."

But Mr. Mai did not explain to Long why the American ghost could not go home again. Maybe it was because he did not know the reason himself—he is, after all, also a city person.

When the American pilot was shot out of the sky, his body was scattered across several bodies of water. And a ghost, as any peasant will tell you, cannot cross a body of water, even a tiny brook, unless his own body is whole. So this American had nowhere to go but to stay where he was. From that point on, Muom Village would have to become his village. His asking for water from the villagers was only a ruse to be allowed inside someone's house. That is, until they decided to build him his own house: the shrine. What the peasants saw when they opened their door to the American was simply his wish to be whole again. They all noticed, for example, that his uniform was untorn, and unstained by blood.

They crossed a truss bridge spanning a deep, leafy ravine, then turned onto a twisting dirt road descending steeply into a narrow valley. Crowding the road on both sides were elephant grass, patches of daisies, mango trees, mangosteens, bamboo, creepers, and a hundred different vines even the locals don't have names for. A copper-colored river appeared and disappeared through the foliage. Shafts of pale light pierced through the bluish-gray clouds, and in the sky someone's kite was spiraling. Now they saw the first villager: a small girl walking toward them alongside an albino buffalo. As they passed, she stared at them blankly and did not wave. Now came the village: thirty houses clustered together, surrounded by rice paddies. The encircling mountains were covered by mist.

■ THE CAVE

for Clayton Eshleman

Because they chased after us for centuries, we had to climb higher and higher, until our village was perched at the top of the highest mountain in the land.

At the very summit of this mountain is a deep cave. It is the mouth of hell itself, and no one has ever been seen to go in there.

There must be many more entrances to hell, some within walking distance of each other perhaps, but we've discovered this one ourselves, and can claim it as our own.

Because we number less than two hundred, a single village on top of a mountain, there's not much we can do against our enemies. And we cannot climb any higher.

We are considered by all (except the Vietnamese) to be the most handsome specimen of the human race: Our men are short, squat, with flattened faces, and our women are tall, hipless, with very high breasts.

Our language is sublime, yet direct. We like to call every-thing by its final condition. Thus a man is *a cadaver*; food, *shit*; a house, *a pile of rubble*.

We have many words for what's on the skin, but almost nothing for what's inside the body. Our names for the male and female sexual organs are interchangeable.

Lest you think our language unusually impoverished, I should add that we can distinguish between a thousand kinds of pota-toes, as well as over a million species of fish. We know a great many words denoting things we have never seen, and a great many more words denoting nothing.

Aside from the bark of an elm tree, which we would swal-low during sad or festive occasions, our only food is called, sim-ply, *the chewed animal*.

We would cook the chewed animal by placing the marinated carcass on the roof of a house for a fortnight. Although highly nutri-tious, the chewed animal has a very subtle flavor, not unlike jas-mine tea. Although no strangers to fire, we use it neither for food preparation nor for illumination. Twice a week we build a series of bonfires, into which we toss most of our meager possessions.

Accumulation implies linear movement, an inching toward the future. But as devotees, or, rather, connoisseurs, of tedium, we want each day to be exactly the same. Fresh beginnings.

Our numerical system consists of a single number. (The invention of a second digit would lead, catastrophically, to verse making and solipsism. A third, eternal torment and vanity. The con-cept of infinity, needless to say, was invented by either a Viet-namese or the devil.)

Our calendar stops at day one.

Our ancestors came to this blighted land from way up north.

Our legends tell of rocks turning into water, of water turning into rocks, and of a single day lasting nearly a lifetime, a paradise lost instead of this unbearably hot land, with its poisonous snakes, large, hairy spiders, scorpions, and tropical fruits.

Traveling is a great curse. Generally speaking, one should never leave one's village. There is nothing to be gained from the next village but a loss of self, anger, and humiliation. Borders are not meant to be crossed (even for licit purposes). It is best to live naturally within one's own confines.

We are citizens of a country called Vietnam, a word most of us can't even pronounce. (Why Vietnam and not China? Why not call it the United States?) Twenty-three men from our village were drafted into their army. Only I came home. I fought against yellow, white, and black men, but the ones I despised most were my own comrades-in-arms—all of them, except for the twenty-two from my village.

People from different villages can never become like brothers. Even if you come from an adjacent village, you already look and sound different from me, pronouncing your e's long instead of short, for example. You will never see me as Thzack, but only as someone who comes from an adjacent village.

When people ask, "What did you see during the war? What was Hanoi like?" I always tell them, "You'd find out by going inside that cave."

The others think I know everything because I've been to a city like Hanoi. An evil, evil place. They assume I've been inside the cave. And they also fear me because they think I've killed a great number of people. A hundred men, maybe a thousand. As far as anyone can remember, there has never been a murder in our village.

While we are certainly capable of evil thoughts, our crimes are invariably petty in nature. We lack both the personal initiative and the social organization to commit decisive acts against God.

Although they said I killed a thousand men, most likely I killed none. I had no idea what I was shooting at. I always aimed my gun too high or too low. It was dust and confusion. Then afterward you gathered the cadavers. Once I snuggled inside a hollowed-out tree trunk during an entire battle.

A person who's been to hell loses his audience, naturally. Either that or he refuses to talk. In any case, we really don't know who's been inside the cave. All we can confirm is that it leads to the core of the earth, where all our dead live.

Most of our hellish stories are spun by inflamed and fiendish individuals whose only experience of the cave came in their sleep or as an act of the imagination.

I've often been tempted to go inside the cave to see the twenty-two men from our village who did not return from the war. We belong to a special club: the only ones to have seen the outside world; the only ones to experience blood, filth, and Hanoi together.

We are also the only ones to have been forced to learn someone else's language.

Their vocabulary has corrupted me irrevocably. Before I learned the Vietnamese word *depressed,* for example, I was never, ever depressed. Likewise, *liver.* It was only after I learned this word that I found out I had a damaged liver. *Second helping, garage door, garbage time, megabytes, coupon,* and many other monstrous words have alienated me permanently from my fellow tribes-men.

A Vietnamese does not know what darkness is. With his 40-

watt bulbs, he has allowed day to encroach upon night. His children are born into a world where there's no true night.

Once I made the mistake of telling a Vietnamese about the cave. He laughed noiselessly, slapped me on the back, and said, "If you can see the dead, then you must be dead yourself! You savages go down into a deep cave, where there's no oxygen, and you sweat and sweat, and you get dizzy, and as you're gasping for air, you collapse onto a few bones. These could be dog bones. Or maybe chicken bones. Or maybe the bones from a bat. But you yell out 'Mother!' in ecstasy, because you think these bones are your relatives! Which they are, no doubt, because only another savage would be stupid enough to crawl into a cave leading to the heart of a mountain, where there's no oxygen!"

The hatred of our enemies defines us. If they were to love us completely, we would surely disappear.

The first man who went into the cave was chasing after a chewed animal. He ran after his prey for many days, pursuing the sounds of its hoofs echoing just ahead. They ran deeper and deeper into the mountain. Among the stalactite and stalagmite formations, which at times resembled birds, breasts, angels, and demons, the man also noticed what appeared to be crudely made furniture. The spongy ground was soaked with a suspicious fluid, and littered throughout with uncooked rice, hair, fingernails, foreign banknotes, and pages torn from a dictionary. He entered and exited countless chambers. In one he saw a mound of naked, sleeping men. In another, a talking statue. The light was dim and reddish, and always came from just around the corner.

The man finally cornered his prey. As he raised his spear to kill it, the chewed animal changed into his dead wife, who had died several years earlier. They embraced, their joy deepened by a touch of dread. Their shared memories, once a closed book on the shelf with only its spine exposed, would now be reopened. The husband said, "Let's go home."

The wife answered, "But I can only walk out of here as a chewed animal, not as a person. You must carry me on your shoulder for the entire trip. And you must not let me touch the ground—not even once!—until we reach the mouth of the cave. Only then can I become a woman again."

The man laid his spear down and lifted his wife onto his shoulder, the way you would carry a cadaver.

He whistled happily as he walked, not feeling his burden, but soon the man noticed that there was fresh blood dripping down his back and chest. *Did I spear her? But I don't remember spearing her!* But it was very dark in there, and there was not much oxygen, so he could not think properly.

He tried to talk to her many times, but she never answered him.

After the second day she started to stink terribly.

After the third day her fur was gone.

After the fourth day he was carrying only bones and sinews, with the meat having rotted off.

After the fifth day he was carrying only her spine.

On the sixth day thinking he has been tricked by an evil spirit, he threw the spine to the ground in disgust.

Immediately he saw that he was standing just outside the cave.

From the cave's mouth his wife called out, "Why have you abandoned me?" before disappearing into thin air.

A Vietnamese, lacking any intuitive understanding of natural laws and God's sense of humor, would say the man missed the opportunity to be reunited with his wife by mere seconds. But

God, being more cruel and playful than man, had already come up with a more satisfying ending:

Had the man not hurled his wife's (or the chewed animal's) backbone to the ground, the next day would find him carrying but a single vertebra. And the next day, only a fraction of that. (Our language lacks specific words for what's inside the body.) The next day he would be lugging around but a single cell on his shoulder. And the next day only a fraction of that....

■ DEAD ON ARRIVAL

I cannot wait to tuck an M-16 under my arm and pump a clip into the bodies of my enemies. I can see them falling backward, in slow motion, leaping up a little, from the force of my bullets. Die, Commies, die! Each day I stare at them in the newspaper, lined up in neat rows, some with their clothes blown off, their arms and legs bent at odd angles. I look at their exposed crotches, at their bare feet. (I cannot help myself: If I see a picture of a near-naked person, I look at the crotch first, then the face, if I look at the face.) Their captured weapons are also lined up in neat rows. Our soldiers can be seen standing in the background, neatly dressed, with their boots on. I cannot wait to get me a pair of black boots. Our national anthem begins like this:

> *Citizens, it's time to liberate the country!*
> *Let's go and sacrifice our lives, with no regrets...*

I'm willing to sacrifice my life and limbs for freedom and democracy.

My father is a police colonel. He answers only to Mr. Thieu, our president, and Mr. Ky, our vice president, and Mr. Khiem, our prime minister, and Mr. Loan, his boss. (Yes, that Mr. Loan, the general who shot a Vietcong on TV. The Vietcong was an assassin who had killed many people that day. He was wearing a plaid shirt, a "caro" shirt.) Mr. Loan is very famous, a celebrity in America and in Europe. It's something to be proud of, having a father with a famous boss.

The Vietcong killed two of my uncles: Uncle Bao and Uncle Hiep. They killed my grandfather. That's all they do. Kill! Kill! Kill! They're born to kill. Mr. Thieu said, "Do not listen to what they say, but look at what they do."

My father was born a peasant. He's used to rustic ways. Although we have modern plumbing in our house, he routinely forgets to close the door when he sits on the toilet. If you walk into our house unannounced, you may catch him, just like that!, sitting on the toilet taking a dump with the door open.

My father encourages me to draw. He said, "Draw, Son, you're good!" He gave me a big brown envelope and said, "Remember to save all your drawings."

I would draw certain things over and over. A few months ago I drew tigers. I would draw a tiger over and over. Then I drew cowboys, a gunslinger wearing a plaid shirt (a "caro" shirt) and leather vest. Then I drew tanks, one tank after another. Lately I've been drawing ships.

There is a huge stranded ship in Vung Tau, with its prow stuck in the sand and its tail sticking out into the ocean. Inside this ship there must be thousands of fish that have swum in through the rusty gashes but are now stuck inside this huge stranded ship and cannot get out again.

Whenever I looked into the ocean, I would think, *There, just beyond my sight, is America. If the earth wasn't so round, I would be able to see it.*

The earth is divided into twenty-four time zones.

If you go east, you lose time. If you go west, you gain time.

If you go far enough east, you lose a whole day. If you go far enough west, you gain a whole day.

If you go far enough west you will end up where you started and it will be yesterday.

We have several words for America. We call it "Flag with Flowers." We call it "Beautiful Country." We call it "Country with Many Races."

So-called white Americans are really red (they look red). Black Americans are blue. Red Americans are yellow.

On Nguyen Hue Street is the tallest building in Saigon. I've seen it many times. I'd count: one, two, three, four, five, six, seven, eight, nine, ten, eleven, twelve! That's it: twelve! The tallest building in Vietnam has twelve stories.

I speak five languages. Aside from Vietnamese, I also speak French:

"Foo? Shoo tit shoo? Le! La! Le! La!" Chinese: "Xi xoong! Xoong xi!" and English: "Well well?"

The hardest word to pronounce in the English language is *the*.

When people say "I'm buying a house," what do they mean by that? I mean, what store is big enough to hold a bunch of houses? Or even just one house? And how are you going to take a house home with you after you've bought it?

Although a dragon only has four legs, sometimes, when I drew him, I'd give him two extra legs.

The three nos of Communism: No God! No Country! No Family!

As me and my father were entering a restaurant—a fancy Chinese place where we go to eat lacquered suckling pig and swallow's nest soup—we saw my mother leaving with her new husband. I mean, as my father opened the glass door, we saw her standing right there, with her new husband.

There is a middle-aged Englishman in our neighborhood. He's always walking around, stooping a little—when you are so tall, you should stoop a little—wearing a pale-blue cotton shirt (with four pockets), a pair of gray slacks, and carrying an old leather briefcase. He has deep-set hazel eyes and a nose like a shark's fin. He's married to a Chinese woman and cannot speak Vietnamese. Every time I saw him, I'd say, "Well well?"

If it weren't for the Vietcong, we'd probably be shooting at the Chinese. There are many Chinese in my neighborhood. They have their own schools and like to play basketball. There is a song:

> A Chinese asshole, it's all one and the same.
> The one who doesn't clean his asshole,
> We'll kick back to China.

Chinese movies are the best. I like *The Blind Swordsman*. He's blind and fights with a sword that's more like a meat cleaver. It's only half a sword really. It doesn't matter: If you know what you're doing, you can kill many people with only half a sword, even if you're blind.

In one movie, Bruce Lee, "The Little Dragon," fought a huge black man named Cream Java. I thought, *This is not very realistic, is it? I mean, my man, Bruce Lee, can't even reach this guy's face to punch him in the face.*

When I draw, I usually aim for absolute realism.

My favorite American movie is *Planet of the Apes.*

The best American band is called the Bee Gees. The second best American band is called the Beatles.

The "Country Homies," the hicks, don't listen to American music. They're embarrassed by it. It frightens them. As soon as you push "play," they become disoriented. These hicks, these "Country Homies," only know how to listen to folk opera.

This is how you get a cricket to fight better. You pick him up by one of his whiskers, then you spin him around a bunch of times. This will make him "drunk." You can also hold him inside your palms and blow into his face.

Some trees are so old that their branches sag and sag and sag until they reach the ground and become new trees. These new trees, in turn, also become so old that their branches sag and sag and sag until they reach the ground and become new trees. What you have, then, is an entire forest connected at the top, an upside-down forest, with the first tree in the middle.

Catholics are the best. All the important people are Catholic. The pope is Catholic. The president is Catholic. My father is Catholic. All the saints are Catholic.

There are many Buddhist kids in my school, which is a Catholic school. If their schools were any good, why would they go to a Catholic school?

What's a buddha?

I go to Lasan Taberd, an all-boys school run by Jesuits near Notre Dame Cathedral and JFK Plaza. In the plaza there is a large plaster statue of the Virgin Mary holding a globe with a little cross sticking out of it.

Last week I accidentally dropped all my colored pencils on the floor and Frère Tuan, our teacher, whacked me on the head with a ruler.

I like Frère Tuan. He called me Dinh Bo Linh once in front of the whole class. (My name is Dinh Hoang Linh.)

Dinh Bo Linh ruled from A.D. 968 to 979. He was a village bully before he became a warlord, before he became the emperor. He was known as Dinh the Celestial King.

To the north was China—Sung Dynasty. To the south was Champas—savages.

In front of the palace was a vat of boiling oil. Criminals were thrown into this vat.

This is how he died: Do Thich, a mandarin, dreamed that a star fell into his mouth. He thought this meant that he would become the next emperor.

One night, as Dinh Bo Linh and his son, Dinh Lien, were passed out, drunk, in a courtyard, Do Thich slashed their throats.

As soldiers searched for him, Do Thich hid in the eaves of the house for three days until he became very thirsty and had to climb down for a drink of water.

A concubine saw him do this and went and told General Nguyen Bac, who had Do Thich executed. His corpse was then chopped into tiny pieces and fed to everyone in the capital.

The capital was Hoa Lu.

Everyone loved Dinh Bo Linh. There is a poem about Do Thich:

> A frog at the edge of a pond,
> Hankering for a star.

I told my best friend, Truong, this story, and he said, "Did they eat his hair too?"

"Probably not."

"How about his bones?"

"Just the smaller bones."

"How do you eat bones?"

"You chop them up real fine and cook them for twenty-four hours."

Truong giggled. "How about his little birdie?"

"That they certainly ate."

"You liar!"

Truong said, "A penis is so ugly to look at, so disgusting, so unnatural. Why do we have penises?"

I said, "They may be ugly, but women love to look at them."

"No, they don't!"

"They love to touch them too."

"Who told you?!"

"They like to put it in their mouth!"

"You're sick!"

"I know what I'm talking about."

"Women are disgusted by the penis."

"You're an idiot."

Truong sits behind me in class. One time he said, "You just farted, didn't you?!"

"No, I didn't."

"How come I smelled it?!"

"I don't care what you smelled. I didn't *feel* it."

One of the kids in my class has neither the middle nor ring finger on his left hand. No one really knows what happened. Someone said he picked up his father's hand grenade and it blew his fingers off. Someone else said he lost his fingers in a motorcycle accident. Maybe he was just born that way. When we see him from afar—say, from across the schoolyard—we raise our fist, with index finger and pinkie upturned, to salute him.

There is another weird kid in my class. The skin on his face has the texture of bark and he cannot close his mouth properly. We call this kid "Planet of the Apes."

The Americans have made a special bomb called "Palm." It's like a big vat of boiling oil that they pour from the sky.

At school, during recess, we divide ourselves into gangs and try to kill each other. I have perfected a move: I feign a right jab, spin 360 degrees, and hit my opponent's face—surprise!—with the back of my left fist as it swings around—whack! So far I've connected with three of my enemies. I hit this one kid, Hung, so hard he fell backward and bounced his head on the ground— booink! Ha, ha! Blood was squirting out of his nose. He was taken by cyclo to the hospital, where he was pronounced Dead On Arrival.

Soon people will catch on to this move, which means that I will have to come up with another move.

It's important to overcome one's ignorance: Our cook, who's illiterate, once told me that a person gains exactly one drop of blood per day from eating. "Otherwise," she said, "where would all that blood go?"

She's very stupid, this woman, although an excellent cook. She knows how to make an excellent omelet with ground pork, bean threads, and scallions. She smells like coconut milk. Every now and then I stand near her as she squats on the kitchen floor snapping watercress and peer into her blouse.

I walked into the dining room and saw Sister Lan—that's the cook's name—sitting by herself. She wiped her face with a hand towel and smiled at me. Her eyes were all red. I said, "You're crying!"

"No! No! I'm not crying."

"Your eyes are all red!"

"I was chopping onions!"

I ran out of the dining room, screaming, "Sister Lan is crying! Sister Lan is crying!"

I told my grandmother about it and she said, "She's thinking about her boyfriend."

Once the foreskin of my penis got caught in the zipper of my pants as I was dressing to go to church. I screamed, "Grandmother! Grandmother!" and my grandmother ran over and pulled the zipper down. That was twice as painful as having my dick caught in the first place.

My grandmother is a good Catholic. She paces back and forth in the living room, fingering her rosary while mumbling her prayer— hundreds of Our Fathers and thousands of Ave Marias—as fast as she can.

I only pray when I've lost something. Once I lost a comic book—my Tintin comic book—and God helped me to find it. I mean: He didn't say, "There, there's your comic book," but as soon as I finished praying, I knew that my comic book was under a pile of newspapers in the living room.

My grandmother goes to church twice a day, once at five in the morning and once at three in the afternoon. Sometimes she makes me come along with her.

The worst part about going to church is having to hear the priest talk. You cannot follow him for more than a few seconds. It's very hot in there. You look around and all the people are fanning themselves, some with their eyes closed.

Father Duong can go on and on and on: "Charity is the key, a camel cannot walk through it....Thirty milch camels with their colts, forty kine and ten bulls, forty she-asses and ten foals....The Lord will give thee a trembling heart, the sole of your foot will not know rest....And so many cows besides?"

A whale spat Jonah out into the desert. It was noon. The sun was blazing.

Jesus felt sorry for Jonah and gave him a gourd for shade.

Jonah slept under this shade.

When Jonah woke up, he was no longer in the shade because the sun had moved.

When Jonah became angry, Jesus said, "And so many cows besides?"

At the end of each sermon, Father Duong always says, "O Merciful Father, please bring peace to this wretched land." That's when you know it's almost time to go home.

As Father Duong walks toward the door, he shakes a metal canister at everyone. That's "holy water."

My patron saint, Saint Martin de Porres, was a black man.

Many beggars stand by the door outside the church. Once I saw my grandmother put a 200-dong bill into a blind man's upturned fedora, then fumble inside it for change totaling 150 dong.

I often think about getting married when I'm in church. About how I'll have to walk down the aisle in front of everyone. I'm not sure I'll be able to do that. I mean, what if you trip and fall as you're walking down the aisle?

To kiss a girl would be like eating ice cream. Her lips will be cold. Her teeth will be cold.

To kiss a girl would be like eating ice cream with strawberries, with the pips from the strawberries getting stuck between your teeth.

My father said, "Women are like monkeys. If you're nice to them, they'll climb all over you."

There's a saying: A French house, an American car, a Japanese wife, Chinese food.

My grandmother has told me this one story over and over (usually when we're having fish for dinner): During the famine of 1940, when the Japanese invaded, the villagers in Bui Chu, her home village, would place a carved wooden fish on the dinner table at mealtime "so they could just stare at it."

My grandmother is deaf in one ear because, as a little girl, she punctured an eardrum with a twig when an ant crawled inside her ear canal.

My grandmother said to me, "Are you going to be a priest when you grow up?"

My grandmother was trying to teach me how to tie my shoes. It's the hardest thing in the world, tying your shoes. I could never figure it out. My father screamed, his face red, "You're an idiot! An idiot!"

I would think about shooting my father, only to have to force myself to think, *I do not want to shoot my father.* Then I would think, once more, about shooting my father, only to have to force myself to think, again, *I do not want to shoot my father.*

■ CHOPPED STEAK MOUNTAIN

From the top of Chopped Steak Mountain, you can see everything: Tibet; the next mountain; Ypsilanti, Michigan; and, on a clear, sunny day, the Jefferson Memorial in Washington, D.C.

Three kinds of palm trees on Chopped Steak Mountain: coconut (to drink), betel (to chew), and rattan (to make furniture with).

An awesome variety of edible animals on Chopped Steak Mountain: hedgehogs, boa constrictors, mongooses, howling monkeys.... Although edible, they ain't too easy to catch. That's why I subsist on a diet of bananas and coconuts.

I live in this hut here, beneath this banyan tree. There's nothing inside it but a cot and a rifle. The mud walls are decorated with pages torn from a Sears catalog. Just looking at this lawn mower can bring tears to my eyes. There's a gargling brook nearby where

I perform my ablutions. I wash a hundred times a day, just to cool off.

You don't need a fancy wardrobe in this weather. No winter coats. No three-piece suits. No hats, gloves, or socks. No pants, actually. If you walk around with all your gear hanging out, no one says shit.

There are no other live souls on top of Chopped Steak Mountain but me.

During the day, I wander in the forest and dig up the odd cassava and eat it. I climb a tall tree and just perch on it for a while. I never enter the forest at night. Too many eyes in the forest at night. Lots of dead souls on Chopped Steak Mountain.

The light slanting through the trees is most beautiful at dusk. Everything is bathed in a pink glow. The brook is aquamarine.

There is this peculiar monkey in the forest. They should name it after me; I discovered it. What it is, is a chameleon monkey. Sometimes it has black limbs, a white head, and a brown body. At other times, brown limbs, a black head, and a white body. I've seen it switch colors right in front of my eyes. Each time it spots me from afar it grabs its dick and jabbers on in monkey gibberish.

The ghosts are just apparitions and I don't pay them no mind. They're just phantoms.

One time I found a ghost napping on the ground. His cammies

were caked in red and brown. He heard me coming, woke up, snapped a salute, and shouted: "USMC! First Marine Division! 'Mike' Company! Third Battalion! Second Regiment! Fourth Platoon! Fifth Squad!"

I've found out on another occasion that this ghost's name is Chuck.

I sit down on this burnt log to write myself a postcard: "*Au contraire*, mother, I'm still alive. I hope you are too. I don't know what year it is in Kentucky, but here it's always 1969, the year of the *White Album*. Until I hear from you, that's a joke, say hello to my sweetheart, another joke. Before I enlisted, I politely asked Janny to put on her wet and wily birthday suit to take a dip in the golden pond with me, but the bitch had the balls to turn me down. I love you, anyway."

I wrote that postcard in my head because I had no pen to write with. I write a postcard a day. I've penned at least a million postcards during my time on Chopped Steak Mountain.

Here's how I fish: I cut a finger and dip it in the brook. A blue fish comes up and bites it, hard!, but it's well worth it. Stubborn and stupid, the fish won't let go even as I yank its wiggly ass out of the water. Sometimes, though, my bleeding finger droops and drools in the brook for hours on end, wasting all that blood, with nothing to show for it.

There is no salt or sugar on Chopped Steak Mountain. What I miss most is ketchup. Mustard also. The cheap, yellow kind. What

I wouldn't do for a nice c-rat of ham and lima beans. Good Lord! The good times now seem better and the bad times not so bad.

I came here on a 707, with a camera slung around my neck. I was only twenty-one years old then. When we sighted land, I thought, *What a beautiful country!* I also thought they were going to shoot us right out of the sky. As I deplaned the heat slapped me on the face. Why didn't they tell me about this frigging heat?!

When I first came here, I thought, *Let's hope the changes this place makes on me will be minimal, and I can go home as my true self.*

But what began as an interruption of my life has turned into my life. Now I would sit on top of a tree and think, I do not care where I am. I have no memories. I was never born in Kentucky.

Every now and then a plane flies over, always an airliner, never a Huey or a Chinook, and I aim my M-16 at its gleaming fuselage, just in jest, and make popping sounds with my mouth. *Pop! Pop! Pop! Pop!* I ain't got no bullets left.

I ain't got no teeth left either. They rotted off years ago. They hurt so bad at one point I thought my skull was rotting.

Should a Via Kong be ambling up this way, I'd level my rifle at him, *Hello, Charlie!*, but, like I said, I ain't got no bullets left.

Halfway down the mountain, there are these houses on stilts, a village inhabited by montagnards. That's a French word, meaning "mountain retards."

Once I did venture halfway down the mountain. I was hiding in the bush, watching the montagnard ladies dip their boobs into the gargling water. I became so vexed and sorrowful I had to high-tail my ass up the craggy mountain before I did something unwholesome. Never again.

Janny, who must be wrinkly by now, is most likely a grandmother. Maybe you're dead already. I came so close to knowing you. You bit me like a blue fish, but you let go of my finger when I tried to lift you out of the water.

All the ladies come back, the girlfriends, the whores, even those glimpsed just once on the streets, one by one, when I sleep alone at night.

I sleep inside this parachute. The mosquitoes are the size of woodpeckers on Chopped Steak Mountain.

One night, as I was lying inside my parachute reciting the streets of my hometown: Melody Lane, Lily Pad Circle, Baseline Drive, Telegraph Road, I heard a loud snoring sound. I went on reciting: Yelling Boulevard, Hunting Pack Street, Frog Pond Drive… but the snoring got louder and louder. It must have come from the biggest set of lungs in the world. I wasn't going to give in. I started screaming: Square Deal Road! Lick Skillet Drive! Possum Road! Greenback Street! The snoring stopped.

This morning I saw Chuck sleeping on the ground but he did not get up to salute me. I squatted down next to his head and was surprised to notice that he was old, like me, and not a young soldier. He had a hurt, sorrowful expression, with some accusation in it. His mouth was wide open and his eyes were slightly open.

About eight miles from here, in a part of the woods I never go into, is my downed helicopter. I was a Scarface, with more than three hundred missions to my credit. I worked the Delta to the DMZ. Every now and then I would manage to be at 1st MAW headquarters with enough time for a lunch break. The chow was fantastic: thick, juicy steaks; baked potatoes with sour cream; apple pie; and vanilla ice cream.

A hilarious memory: I once saw a Filipino queer impersonating Mick Jagger at a USO show. He was good too. The shit you remember.

The capital of Kentucky is Frankfort, population: 20,000. There was a nice tavern at the corner of Broadway and Madison, where you could get an excellent roast beef sandwich for 89 cents.

My favorite sport is football. My second favorite sport is baseball. I was a pitcher in high school, with a fastball that topped off at eighty miles an hour.

The stadium in Lexington can hold seventy thousand people. I was there at least a dozen times. We always sat in the cheapest seats, me and my father.

My old phone number is 732-0806. Janny's phone number is 922-7908.

I was only supposed to be here for eleven months and twenty days.

I was not born in this country, but I will die in this country.

About the Author

Artist and writer **Linh Dinh** was born in Saigon in 1963; came to the United States in 1975; and after twenty-four years away from Vietnam, returned to live in Saigon in 1998. Dinh is the author of a chapbook of poems, *Drunkard Boxing* (Singing Horse Press, 1998), and the editor of a short story anthology, *Night, Again: Contemporary Fiction from Vietnam* (Seven Stories Press, 1996). In 1993 he was the recipient of a Pew Charitable Trust fellowship for his poetry. His stories, poems, and translations have appeared in recent issues of the *Threepenny Review, New American Writing, Chicago Review, Sulfur, Denver Quarterly, American Poetry Review, New York Stories,* and *VOLT,* among other journals. His poem, "The Most Beautiful Word," has been anthologized in *Best American Poetry 2000.*